W9-CBZ-226

JUL – – 2014

ALSO BY RIVKA GALCHEN

Atmospheric Disturbances

AMERICAN INNOVATIONS

AMERICAN INNOVATIONS

RIVKA GALCHEN

FARRAR, STRAUS AND GIROUX   NEW YORK

Farrar, Straus and Giroux
18 West 18th Street, New York 10011

Copyright © 2014 by Rivka Galchen
All rights reserved
Printed in the United States of America
First edition, 2014

These stories previously appeared, in slightly different form, in the following publications: *Harper's Magazine* ("Once an Empire"), *The New Yorker* ("The Lost Order," "The Region of Unlikeness," "Sticker Shock" as "Appreciation," "The Entire Northern Side Was Covered with Fire," and "The Late Novels of Gene Hackman"), *Open City* ("Wild Berry Blue"), and *The Walrus* ("Real Estate").

Library of Congress Cataloging-in-Publication Data
Galchen, Rivka.
    [Short stories. Selections]
    American innovations / Rivka Galchen. — First edition.
        pages   cm
    ISBN 978-0-374-28047-5 (Hardcover) — ISBN 978-0-374-71170-2 (Ebook)
    I. Title.

PS3607.A4116 A6 2014
813'.6—dc23

                                                                2013039912

Designed by Jonathan D. Lippincott

Farrar, Straus and Giroux books may be purchased for educational, business, or promotional use. For information on bulk purchases, please contact the Macmillan Corporate and Premium Sales Department at 1-800-221-7945, extension 5442, or write to specialmarkets@macmillan.com.

www.fsgbooks.com
www.twitter.com/fsgbooks • www.facebook.com/fsgbooks

10 9 8 7 6 5 4 3 2 1

For Georgie and Yosefa

CONTENTS

THE LOST ORDER

I was at home, not making spaghetti. I was trying to eat a little less often, it's true. A yogurt in the morning, a yogurt at lunchtime, ginger candies in between, and a normal dinner. I don't think of myself as someone with a "weight issue," but I had somehow put on a number of pounds just four months into my unemployment, and when I realized that this had happened—I never weigh myself; my brother just said to me, on a visit, "I don't recognize your legs"—I wasn't happy about it. Although maybe I was happy about it. Because at least I had something that I knew it wouldn't be a mistake to really dedicate myself to. I could be like those people who by trying to quit smoking or drinking manage to fit an accomplishment, or at least an attempt at an accomplishment, into every day. Just by aiming to not do something. This particular morning, there was no yogurt left for my breakfast. I could go get some? I could treat myself to maple. Although the maple yogurt was always full cream. But maybe full cream was fine, because it was just a tiny—

My phone is ringing.

The caller ID reads "Unavailable."

I tend not to answer calls identified as Unavailable. But sometimes Unavailable shows up because someone is calling from, say, the hospital.

"One garlic chicken," a man's voice is saying. "One side of salad, with the ginger-miso dressing. Also one white rice.

White, not brown. This isn't for pickup," he says. "It's for delivery."

He probably has the wrong number, I figure. I mean, of course he has the wrong—

"Not the lemon chicken," he is going on. "I don't want the lemon. What I want—"

"OK. I get it—"

"Last time you delivered the wrong thing—"

"Lemon chicken—"

"Garlic chicken—"

"OK—"

"I know you," he says.

"What?"

"Don't just say 'OK' and then bring me the wrong order. OK, OK, OK. Don't just say 'OK.' " He starts dictating his address. I have no pencil in hand.

"OK," I say. "I mean, all right." I've lost track of whether it was the lemon chicken or the garlic he wanted. Wanting and not wanting. Which tap is hot and which is cold. I still have trouble with left and right.

"How long?" he asks.

"Thirty minutes?"

He hangs up.

Ack. Why couldn't I admit that I wasn't going to be bringing him any chicken at all? Now I'm wronging a hungry man. One tries not to do too many wrong things in life. But I can't call him back: he's Unavailable!

Just forget it.

·

Forgetting is work, though. I returned to not making spaghetti, a task to which I had added not setting out to buy yogurt. Then it struck me that getting dressed would be a good idea. It was 10:40 a.m. Early for chicken. Yes, I should and would

get dressed. Unfortunately, on the issue of getting dressed I
consistently find myself wishing that I were a man. I don't
mean that in an ineluctable gender disturbance way, it's not
that; it's that I think I would have an easier time choosing an
outfit. Though having a body is problematic no matter what.
Even for our dog. One summer we thought we would do her a
favor by shaving her fur, but then afterward she hung her head
and was inconsolable. Poor girl. The key is to not have time to
think about your body, and dogs—most dogs anyhow—have
a lot of free time. So do I, I guess. Although, I don't *feel* like I
have a lot of time; I feel constantly pressed for time; even though
when I had a job, I felt like I had plenty of time. But even then
getting dressed was difficult. For a while it was my conviction
that pairing tuxedo-like pants with any of several inexpensive
white T-shirts would solve the getting-dressed problem for me
for at least a decade, maybe for the rest of my life. I bought
the tuxedo-like pants! Two pairs. And some men's under-
shirts. But it turned out that I looked even more sloppy than
usual. And by sloppy I mostly just mean female, with curves,
which can be OK, even great, in many circumstances, sure, but
a tidy look for a female body, feminine or not feminine, is elusive and unstable. Dressing as a woman is like working with
color instead of with black and white. Or like drawing a circle
freehand. They say that Giotto got his job painting St. Peter's
based solely on the pope's being shown a red circle he'd painted
with a single brushstroke. That's how difficult circles are. In
the seven hundred years since Giotto, probably still—
    I found myself back in the kitchen, still not making spa-
ghetti, and wearing a T-shirt. Not the one I had woken up in,
but still a T-shirt that would be best described as pajamas and
that I wasn't feeling too good or masculine or flat-chested in,
either. Giotto? It was 11:22 a.m. Making lemon chicken for
that man would have been a better way to spend my time, I
thought. Or garlic chicken. Whichever. I felt as if there were

some important responsibility that I was neglecting so wholly that I couldn't even admit to myself that it was there. Was I really taking that man's delivery order so seriously?

At least I wasn't eating.

I decided to not surf the Internet.

Then to not watch a television show.

Hugging my favorite throw pillow, I lay down on the sofa, and thought, Just count backward from one hundred. This is something I do that calms me down. What's weird is that I don't recall ever having made it to the number one. Sometimes I fall asleep before I reach one—that's not so mysterious—but more often I just get lost. I take some sort of turn away from counting, without realizing it, and only then, far away even from whatever the turn was, do I realize I am elsewhere.

The throw pillow has matryoshka dolls on it. I started counting down. Ninety-six, ninety-five, ninety-four . . .

The phone is ringing.

It's Unavailable.

I hate my phone. I hate all phones.

Why should I have to deal with this hungry man's problems, these problems that stem from a past to which I don't belong? Not my fucking jurisdiction.

Although admittedly, the fact that our paths are now entangled—that part kind of is my fault.

"OK?" I say, into the phone.

"I think I know where it is," a familiar male voice says.

"It's not even on its way yet," I confess. "I'm sorry."

"What's not on its way? Are you asleep?"

I locate the voice more precisely. The voice belongs to my husband.

"Sorry, sorry. I'm here now."

"I'm saying I think I know where it is. I think I lost it when I was in the courtyard with Monkey, tossing tennis balls for her." Our dog's name is Monkey. One of the reasons I was lonelier than usual was that Monkey was on a kind of dog holiday in the country, with my in-laws. "My hands were really cold. I had bought an icy water bottle."

"OK," I say.

"You know how it is, when your hand gets cold; your fingers shrink. So maybe that's when the ring fell off. I'm almost sure of it. It's supposed to rain later today, and I'm worried the rain will just wash the ring right into a gutter. I'm sorry to put this on you, but would you mind taking a look around for it?"

He is talking about: a couple of weeks earlier I had very briefly gone away, to my uncle's funeral, and when I returned, my husband was no longer wearing his wedding ring. It's such an unimportant thing that to be honest, I didn't even notice he was no longer wearing it. And he hadn't noticed, either. We're not symbol people. We didn't realize that his ring was gone until we were at dinner with a friend visiting from Chicago and she asked to see both of our rings. Then my husband was a little weird about it. I guess he had simultaneously known and not known. Meaning he had known. A part of him had. And had worried enough about it to pretend that it hadn't happened. Poor guy.

"I'm not going to go look for it," I find myself saying into the phone. It's not really a decision, it's more like a discovery. I'm not going to be a woman hopelessly searching for a wedding ring in a public courtyard. Even if the situation does not in fact carry the metaphorical weight it misleadingly seems to carry. Still no. I had recently seen a photograph of Susan Sontag wearing a bear costume but with a serious expression on her face; you could see that she felt uneasy.

"Just go and even try *not* looking for it," my husband is saying. "Just give the courtyard a little visit. Please."

"There's no way it's still—"

"You really can't do this one little thing?"

"This is my fault?"

"I'm on hour twenty-nine of my shift here."

"I'm not doing nothing," I say. I find I've neither raised nor lowered my voice, though I feel like I have done both. "You think I'm not capable, but that's not right. You just don't understand my position. You see me all wrong. It's not fair, it's not right—"

"I'm so sorry, my love," he is saying. His voice has hairpin-turned to tender. Which is alarming. "I'm on your side," he says. "I really do love you so much. You know that, right? You know I love you so much."

We hadn't always conversed in a way that sounded like advanced ESL students trying to share emotions, but recently that was happening to us; I think we were just trying to keep a steady course through an inevitable and insignificant strait in our relationship.

"I'm sorry, Boo," I say. "I'm the one who should apologize." I am suddenly missing him very badly, as if I have been woken from one of those dreams where the dead are still with us. Being awake feels awful. I language along, and then at some point in my ramblings he says to me, "I have to go now," and then he is gone.

·

The daytime hours in this neighborhood belong almost exclusively to deliverymen and nannies. The deliverymen are all men. And the nannies are all women. And the women are all dark-skinned. I had not given much thought to my neighborhood's socioeconomic or gender clustering before I became a daylight ghost. I mean, sure, I knew about it vaguely, but there it was—under cover of day, one saw, or at least it seemed as if one saw, that decades of feminism and civil rights advances had never happened. This was appalling. Yet there was not no comfort for me in the idea that men had strong calves, and carried things, and that it was each toddler's destiny to fall in love with another woman. Was it my fault that these feelings lived inside me? Maybe.

I had not always—had not even long—been a daylight ghost, a layabout, a *mal pensant*, a vacancy, a housewife, a person foiled by the challenge of getting dressed and someone who considered eating less a valid primary goal. I had been a fairly busy environmental lawyer, an accidental expert of sorts in toxic mold litigation—litigation concerning alleged damage to property and persons by reason of exposure to toxic mold. I handled the first toxic mold case that came into the firm, so when the second case turned up, shortly thereafter, I was the go-to girl. A Texas jury had made an award of thirty-two million dollars in a case in 2001, and that had set a lot of hearts to dreaming. But the Texas case was really an insurance case, and so not a precedent for toxic mold cases. Most people don't understand that. An insurance company had failed to pay promptly for repairs to leaking pipes in a twenty-two-room mansion that subsequently became moldy; all claims relating to personal injuries from toxic mold were dismissed, and an award was made only for property damage, punitive damages, mental anguish, and to cover plaintiff's legal fees of nearly nine million dollars. But since the case was on the evening news, it was, predictably, radically misrepresented. Hence, toxic mold–litigation fever. It has been established that mold, like dust, is environmentally pervasive; some of us are allergic to some molds, just as some of us are allergic to dust, though whether any mold can damage our health in a lasting or severe way is unlikely, and certainly not scientifically proven. Also clear is that basic maintenance is an essential duty of a property owner. But beyond that . . . I handled quite a large number of mold cases. I filled out the quiet fields of forms. I dispatched environmental testers. The job was more satisfying than it sounds, I can tell you. To have any variety of expertise, and to deploy it, can feel like a happy dream.

But one day I woke up and heard myself saying, I am a fork being used to eat cereal. I am not a spoon. I am a fork. And I can't help people eat cereal any longer.

I judged my sentiment foolish, sure, but it captained me nevertheless. I laid no plan, but that afternoon I found myself saying to the managing partner, "I'm afraid I'll need to tender my resignation." I used that word, "tender."

I could have rescinded all those words, of course.

But that night, after the tender word, I said to Boo, "I think I'm leaving my job."

He set down his handheld technology.

"Don't worry," I said. "I'll find some other work."

"No, it's really OK," he said. "You don't have to work at all. If you don't want to. Or you could work at a bakery. Why not? You'll figure it out. Under no time pressure, OK? I like my work. We can live from that."

My husband is a pretty understanding guy; nevertheless, I found myself thinking of an old Japanese movie where the father gets stomach cancer but the family keep it a secret from him, and are all just very kind to him. "But you might wake up one day and not like your work anymore," I said.

"That's not going to happen to me," he said. "I'm just not like that." Then he added, "I could see you were unhappy. I could see that before you could. Honestly, I feel relieved."

•

When the phone rings again—Unavailable—I pick it up right away. I had been so childish about not wanting to go look for the ring; I would tell Boo that I would go look for the ring, and then I would do that, I would go and look for it.

"Fifty-five minutes," he says.

"I'm so sorry, I—"

"You said half an hour. It's about expectations and promises. You don't have to make these promises. But you do. You
leave people expecting. Which is why you're not just a loser
working a shit job but also a really terrible person, the very
worst kind, the kind who needs everyone to think she's so nice.
I never found you attractive. I never trusted you. You say, Yes,
this, and I'm Sorry, that, and Oops, Really Sorry, and We Just
Want to Do What Makes You Happy, but who falls for that? I
don't fall for it. I'm the one who sees who you really are—"

"I think you—"

"Why do you apologize and giggle all the time? To every
guy the same thing. Why do you wear that silver leotard and
that ridiculous eye shadow? Your breasts look uneven in that
leotard. You know what you look like? You look like a whore.
Not like an escort or a call girl. You look like a ten-dollar
blow job. If you think you're ever going to pass in this city as
anything other than just one more whore-cunt—"

I hang up the phone.

I turn off the phone.

I pour myself a glass of water, but first I spill it and then I
altogether drop it, and then I clean that up poorly. I don't even
own a silver leotard. Yet I had been called out by a small and
omniscient God. I was going to be punished, and swiftly. I
put on my husband's boots and his raincoat, unintentionally
creating a rubbery analogue of the clean and flat-chested look
I have for years longed for. I left the apartment and headed out
to the courtyard, a few blocks away; I wasn't going to come
back without that ring.

·

When I get to the courtyard, I see that it is not really a courtyard, but just some concrete and a few picnic tables at the
windy base of the tallest building in the neighborhood. Thinking of it as a courtyard—I guess that was a fantasy on which

my husband and I had subconsciously colluded. I do see something glinting in the midday sun; it proves to be a silvery gum wrapper. There's not even a coin on the ground. Bear suit, I'm thinking. It starts to drizzle. Then I remember: doormen are more than just people one feels one has failed to entertain. If I were in a so-called courtyard, and I found a band of gold that didn't belong to me—

Between the doorman and me, there at his desk, are two women. The women are dark-skinned; they are both wearing brown; they are wearing, I realize on delay, UPS uniforms. One of them is also wearing a fleecy brown vest. "The guy was totally whacked," the vested one says.

I feel somewhat bad because I find I am staring at these women's asses (I think of that word as the most gentle and affectionate of the options) and I feel somewhat good because both of the asses are so attractive, though they are quite different: one is juvenile and undemanding, and the other is unembarrassedly space-occupying and reminiscent somehow of gardening—of bending over and doing things. The pants are nicely tight-fitting. I do know that I—and really everyone—am not supposed to think this way about women, or for that matter about men, because, I guess the argument goes, it reduces people to containers of sexual possibility. But I'm not sure that's quite what is going on. Maybe I just think these women have solved the getting dressed problem. "I think that was his friend," one of them says, "writing down the license plate number of the truck."

"Was someone bothering you guys?" I find myself interjecting. "This is a weirdly rough neighborhood. Even as it's kind of a nice neighborhood, it's also sort of a rough one—"

"Every neighborhood is rough today—"

"It's iPhone day—"

The UPS women have turned and opened their circle to me.

"They've ordered two million iPhones—"

"Someone in my neighborhood already got stabbed over a delivery."

"I hate phones," I offer. "I really hate them."

"There's no Apple in Russia," the doorman says. "You can sell the phones to a Russian for fourteen hundred dollars. You buy them for six hundred; you sell them for fourteen hundred."

"Delivery must be terrifying," I say to the women. "You never know what's up with the person on the other side of the door. It's like you knock on your own nightmare."

"People love their iPhones," the vested deliverywoman says. "My daughter says it's like they would marry their iPhones."

I keep not asking about Boo's ring. "I've never seen a woman working UPS delivery before," I say. "And now here you are— two of you at once. I feel like I'm seeing a unicorn. Or the Loch Ness monster. Maybe both, I guess."

There's a bit of a quiet then.

"They don't normally travel in twos," the doorman says. "It's only because today is considered dangerous."

"There's at least a hundred of us," the unvested woman says, shrugging.

"Not too many, but some."

"Good luck," the doorman is saying.

The women are walking away.

Now it's just me and the doorman. I am back in the familiar world again. I feel compelled to hope that he finds me attractive, and I feel angry at him, as if he were responsible for that feeling, and I find myself unzipping my husband's raincoat and pushing back the hood, like one of those monkeys whose ovulation is not concealed. I'm looking for, I imagine myself saying to this man, a wedding ring. Oh, he says, You're all looking for rings.

There was no ring there. But you saw a unicorn today, I

remind myself. That's something. It's all about keeping busy. We can just buy another ring. Why didn't we think of that earlier? The old ring cost, maybe, three hundred dollars. We could buy a new one, nothing wrong with that, no need to think it means something it doesn't, though it would mean something nice to have it again, I think to myself, as I find an appealing empty table in the back corner of a Peruvian chicken joint, where I order french fries. Some people save their marriages— not that our marriage needs saving, not that it's in danger, one can't be seduced by the semantically empty loss of a ring, I remind myself—by having adventures together. We could pull a heist. Me and Boo. Boo and . . . well, we'd have some Bonnie and Clyde–type name, just between ourselves. We could heist a UPS truck full of iPhones. On a rural delivery route. The guns wouldn't need to be real, definitely not. We could then move to another country. An expensive and cold one where no one comes looking and where people leave their doors unlocked because wealth is distributed so equitably. This is not my kind of daydream, I think. This is not my sort of reverie. It is someone else's. Maybe that's fine. I was never a Walter Mitty myself. Though I consistently fell in love with and envied that type. But a Walter Mitty can't be married to a Walter Mitty. It doesn't work. There is a maximum allowance of one Walter Mitty per household. That's just how it goes.

·

"Why is your phone off? Where were you?"

I guess hours have passed. Boo is back home. It's dark out.

"I got scared," I say. "I was getting scary phone calls. I'm sorry. I'm really sorry."

There's opened mail on the table.

Boo says, "Look, I know there's something important that you haven't told me."

My body seems to switch climates. It must be the unbreathing raincoat.

"I know you're scared," he is saying. "I know you're scared of lots of things. I don't want to catch you out. I'm tired of catching out. I don't want to be a catcher-outer. I just want to be told. Just tell me the thing that you've been hiding from me. This could be a good day for us. You could tell me, and then I will feel like I can begin to trust you more again, because I'll know you can tell me things even when it is scary and difficult to tell."

I see that along with the mail, there is a shoebox full of my papers on the table. "I was just out," I hear myself saying. Is this something to do with the guy calling for delivery? "I was just lonely in the house, and spooked, and so I went out," I go on. "I had a salad. I guess various things happen in a day. I guess one can always share more. But I can't think of anything I would call a secret."

There is a long pause now. As if, I'm thinking, I'd made an awkward, outsize observation, like calling *him* the Loch Ness monster, or a unicorn. He is my unicorn, though. I forgot that I used to say that; that's how I felt falling in love with him, as if I'd found a creature of myth. He was less practical then, more dreamy. He had an old belt with a little pony on it; the pony was always upside down.

"Please," he says. "I'm asking as nicely as I can. Don't you have something you want to say to me?"

"I went out and looked for the ring," I say. "I wanted to tell you that. I didn't find the ring. But I did look for it. We should just buy another one."

"A severance check arrived for you," he says. "Actually, I've found three of your severance checks."

"That's odd," I am saying.

"None of them have been cashed, of course."

The unicorn suddenly has a lot to say. Why couldn't I just

tell him that I was fired? he is saying. Or he is saying something like that. I really and truly and genuinely don't know what he is talking about. I am saying that I said I resigned because I did resign. I really do remember using that word, "tender," in offering my resignation. And there's been a lot of misdirected mail lately, I say. Even misdirected calls. I have been meaning to mention that to him.

He is saying that lots of people lie, but why do I tell lies that don't even help me? It's just fucking weird, he is saying. Also something about the rent, and about health insurance. "And I don't even really care that much about any of those things," he says. "I just care that even when you're in this room with me, you're not here. Even when you're here, you're gone. You're just in some la-la. Go back out the door and it'll be just the same: you're somewhere else and I'm here alone—"

I think this goes on for quite a while. Accusations. Analyses. I feel something like a kind of happiness, shy but arrived. A faint fleeting smile, in front of the firing squad. All my vague and shifting self-loathings are streamlining into brightly delineated wrongs. This particular trial—it feels so angular and specific. So lovable. At least lovable by me. Maybe I'm the dreamer in the relationship after all. Maybe I'm the man.

THE REGION OF UNLIKENESS

Some people would consider Jacob a physicist, others might say he's a philosopher, or simply a "time expert," but I tend to think of him in less reverent terms. Though not terms of hatred. Ilan used to call Jacob "my cousin from Outer Swabia." That obscure little joke, which I heard Ilan make a number of times, probably without realizing how many times he'd made it before, always seemed to me to imply a distant blood relation between the two of them. I guess I had the sense (back then) that Jacob and Ilan were shirttail cousins of a kind. But later I came to believe, at least intermittently, that actually Ilan's little phrase was both a misdirection and a sort of clue, one that hinted at an enormous secret, one that they'd never let me in on. Not a dully personal secret, like an affair or a small crime or, say, a missing testicle—but a scientific secret, that rare kind of secret that, in our current age, still manages to bend our knee.

I met Ilan and Jacob by chance. Sitting at the table next to mine in a small Moroccan coffee shop on the Upper West Side, they were discussing *Wuthering Heights* too loudly, having the kind of reference-laden conversation that unfortunately never fails to attract me. Jacob looked about forty-five; he was overweight, he was munching obsessively on these unappetizing green leaf-shaped cookies, and he kept saying "obviously." Ilan was good-looking, and he said that the tragedy of Heathcliff was that he was essentially, on account of his lack of property rights, a woman. Jacob then extolled Catherine's proclaiming, "I am Heathcliff." Something about passion was said. And about digging up graves. And a bearded young man next to them moved to a more distant table. Jacob and Ilan talked on, unoffended, praising Brontë, and at some point Ilan added, "But since Jane Austen's usually the token woman on university syllabi, it's understandable if your average undergraduate has a hard time shaking the idea that women are half-wits, moved only by the terror that a man might not be as rich as he seems."

Not necessarily warmly, I chimed in with something. Ilan laughed. Jacob refined Ilan's statement to "straight women." Then to straight women "in the Western tradition." Then the three of us spoke for a long time. That hadn't been my intention. But there was something about Ilan—manic, fragile, fidgety, womanizing (I imagined) Ilan—that was all at once like fancy coffee and bright-colored smutty flyers. He had a great deal to say, with a steady gaze into my eyes, about my reading the *New York Post*, which he interpreted as a sign of a highly satiric yet demotically moral intelligence. Jacob nodded. I let the flattery go straight to my heart, despite the fact that I didn't read the *Post*; it had simply been left on my table by a previous customer. Ilan called *Post* writers naive Nabokovs. Yes, I said. The headline, I remember, read "Axis of Weasel." Somehow this led to Jacob's saying something vague about Proust, and violence, and perception.

"Jacob's a boor, isn't he?" Ilan said. Or maybe he said "bore" and I heard "boor" because Ilan's way of talking seemed so antiquated to me. I had so few operating sources of pride at that time. I was tutoring and making my lonely way through graduate school in civil engineering, where my main sense of joy came from trying to silently outdo the boys—they still played video games—in my courses. I started going to that coffee shop every day.

.

Everyone I knew seemed to find my new companions arrogant and pathetic, but whenever they called me, I ran to join them. Ilan and Jacob were both at least twenty years older than me, and they called themselves philosophers, although only Jacob seemed to have an actual academic position, and maybe a tenuous one, I couldn't quite tell. I was happy not to care about those things. Jacob had a wife and daughter, too, though I never met them. It was always just the three of us. We would get together and Ilan would go on about Heidegger and "thrownness," or about Will Ferrell, and Jacob would come up with some way to disagree, and I would mostly just listen and eat baklava and drink lots of coffee. Then we'd go for a long walk, and Ilan might have some argument in defense of, say, fascist architecture, and Jacob would say something about the striated and the smooth, and then a pretty girl would walk by and they would talk about her outfit for a long time. Jacob and Ilan always had something to say, which gave me the mistaken impression that I did, too.

Evenings we'd go to the movies, or eat at an overpriced restaurant, or lie around Ilan's spacious and oddly neglected apartment. He had no bed frame, nothing hung on the walls, and in his bathroom there was just a single white towel and a TWA mini toothbrush. But he had a two-hundred-dollar pair of leather gloves. One day, when I went shopping with the two of them, I found myself buying a simple striped sweater so expensive that I couldn't get to sleep that night.

None of this behavior—the laziness, the happiness, the subservience, even the pretentiousness—was "like me." I was accustomed to using a day planner and eating my lunch alone, in fifteen minutes; I bought my socks at street fairs. But when I was with them, I felt like, well, a girl. Or "the girl." I would see us from the outside and recognize that I was, in an old-fashioned and maybe even demeaning way, the sidekick, the mascot, the decoration; it was thrilling. And it didn't hurt that Ilan was so generous with his praise. I fixed his leaking shower, and he declared me a genius. Same when I roasted a chicken with lemons. When I wore orange socks with jeans, he kissed my feet. Jacob told Ilan to behave with more dignity.

It's not as if Jacob wasn't lovable in his own abstruse and awkward way. I admired how much he read—probably more than Ilan, certainly more than me (he made this as clear as he could)—but Jacob struck me as pedantic, and I thought he would do well to button his shirts a couple of buttons higher. Once we were all at the movies—I had bought a soda for four dollars—and Jacob and I were waiting wordlessly for Ilan to return from the men's room. It felt like a very long wait. Several times I had to switch the hand I was holding the soda in because the waxy cup was so cold. "He's taking such a long time," I said, and shrugged my shoulders, just to throw a ripple into the strange quiet between us.

"You know what they say about time," Jacob said idly. "It's what happens even when nothing else does."

"OK," I said. The only thing that came to my mind was the old joke that time flies like an arrow and fruit flies like a banana. I couldn't bear to say it. It was as if without Ilan we couldn't even pretend to have a conversation.

Though there were, I should admit, things about Ilan (in particular) that didn't make me feel so good about myself. For example, once I thought he was pointing a gun at me, but it turned out to be a remarkably good fake. Occasionally when he poured me a drink, he would claim he was trying to poison me. One night I even became very sick, and wondered. Another evening—maybe the only time Jacob wasn't with us; he said his daughter had appendicitis—Ilan and I lay on his mattress watching TV. For years watching TV had made me sick with a sense of dissoluteness, but now suddenly it seemed really great. That night Ilan took hold of one of my hands and started idly to kiss my fingers, and I felt—well, I felt I'd give up the rest of my life just for that. Then Ilan got up and turned off the television. Then he fell asleep, and the hand kissing never came up again.

Ilan frequently called me his dusty librarian. And once he called me his Inner Swabian, and this struck him as very funny, and even Jacob didn't seem to understand why. Ilan made a lot of jokes that I didn't understand. But he had that handsome face, and his pants fit him just so, and he liked to lecture Jacob about how smart I was after I'd, say, nervously folded up my napkin in a way he found charming. I got absolutely no work done while I was friends with those guys. And hardly any reading, either. What I mean to say is that those were the happiest days of my entire life.

.

Then we fell apart. I just stopped hearing from them. Ilan didn't return my calls. I waited and waited. But I was remarkably poised about the whole thing. I assumed that Ilan had simply found a replacement mascot. And that Jacob—in love with Ilan, in his way—hardly registered the swapping out of one girl for another. Suddenly it seemed a mystery to me that I had ever wanted to spend time with them. Ilan was just a charming parrot. And Jacob the parrot's parrot. And if Jacob was married and had a child, wasn't it time for him to grow up and spend his days like a responsible adult? That, anyway, was the disorganized crowd of my thoughts. Several months passed, and I almost convinced myself that I was glad to be alone again. I took on more tutoring.

Then one day I ran randomly (OK, not so randomly; I was haunting our old spots like the most unredeemed of ghosts) into Jacob.

For the duration of two iced teas, Jacob sat with me, repeatedly noting that sadly, he really had no time at all, he really would have to be going. We chatted about this and that and about the tasteless yet uncanny ad campaign for a B movie called *Silent Hill* (the poster image was of a child normal in all respects except for the absence of a mouth), and Jacob went on and on about how much some prominent philosopher adored him, and about how deeply unmutual the feeling was, and about the burden of unsolicited love, until finally, my heart a hummingbird, I asked, "And how is Ilan?"

Jacob's face went the proverbial white. I don't think I'd ever actually seen that happen to anyone. "I'm not supposed to tell you," he said.

Not saying anything seemed my best hope for remaining composed.

"I don't want your feelings to be hurt," Jacob went on. "I'm sure Ilan wouldn't have wanted them hurt, either."

After a long pause, I said, "Jacob, I'm not some disastrous heroine." It was a bad imitation of something Ilan might have said. "Just tell me."

"Well, let's see. He died."

"What?"

"He had, well, so it is, well, he had stomach cancer. Inoperable, obviously. He kept it a secret. Told only family."

I recalled the cousin from Outer Swabia line. Also, I felt certain—somehow really certain—that I was being lied to. That Ilan was actually still alive. Just tired of me. Or something. "He isn't dead," I said, trying to deny the creeping sense of humiliation gathering at my liver's portal vein.

"Well, this is very awkward," Jacob said flatly. "I feel suddenly that my whole purpose on earth is to tell you the news of Ilan—that this is my most singular and fervent mission. Here I am, failing, and yet still I feel as though this job were, somehow, my deepest essence, who I really—"

"Why do you talk like that?" I interrupted. I had never, in all our time together, asked Jacob (or Ilan) such a thing.

"You're in shock—"

"What does Ilan even do?" I asked, ashamed of this kind of ignorance above all. "Does he come from money? What was he working on? I never understood. He always seemed to me like some kind of stranded time traveler, from an era when you really could get away with just being good at conversation—"

"Time traveler. Funny that you say that." Jacob shook extra sugar onto the dregs of his iced tea and then slurped at it. "Ilan may have been right about you. Though honestly I could never see it myself. Well, I need to get going."

"Why do you have to be so obscure?" I asked. "Why can't you just be sincere?"

"Sincere. Huh. Let's not take such a genial view of social circumstances so as to uphold sincerity as a primary value," he said, with affected distraction, stirring his remaining ice with his straw. "Who you really are—very bourgeois myth, that. Obviously an anxiety about social mobility."

I could have cried, trying to control that conversation. Maybe Jacob could see that. Finally, looking at me directly, and with his tone of voice softened, he said, "I really am very sorry for you to have heard like this." He patted my hand in what seemed like a genuine attempt at tenderness. "I imagine I'll make this up to you, in time. But listen, sweetheart, I really do have to head off. I have to pick my wife up from the dentist and my kid from school, and there you go, that's what life is like. I would advise you to seriously consider avoiding it—life, I mean—altogether. I'll call you. Later this week. I promise."

He left without paying.

He had never called me sweetheart before. And he'd never so openly expressed the opinion that I had no life. He didn't phone me that week, or the next, or the one after that. Which was OK. Maybe, in truth, Jacob and I had always disliked each other.

.

I found no obituary for Ilan. If I'd been able to find any official trace of him at all, I think I might have been comforted. But he had vanished so completely that it seemed like a trick. As if for clues, I took to reading the *New York Post*. I learned that professional wrestlers were dying mysteriously young, that baseball players and politicians tend to have mistresses, and that a local archbishop who'd suffered a ski injury was now doing, all told, basically fine. I was fine, too, in the sense that every day I would get out of bed in the morning, walk for an hour, go to the library and work on problem sets, drink tea, eat yogurt and bananas and falafel, avoid seeing people, rent a movie, and then fall asleep watching it.

One afternoon—it was February—a letter addressed to Ilan showed up in my mailbox. It wasn't the first time this had happened; Ilan had often, with no explanation, directed mail to my apartment, a habit I'd assumed had something to do with evading collection agencies. But this envelope had been addressed by hand.

Inside, I found a single sheet of paper with an elaborate diagram in Ilan's handwriting: billiard balls and tunnels and equations heavy with Greek. At the bottom it said, straightforwardly enough, "Jacob will know."

This struck me as a silly, false clue—one that I figured

Jacob himself had sent. I believed it signified nothing. But. My face flushed, and my heart fluttered, and I felt as if I were a morning glory vine in bloom.

I set aside my dignity and called Jacob.

Without telling him why, assuming that he knew, I asked him to meet me for lunch. He excused himself with my-wife-this, my-daughter-that; I insisted that I wanted to thank him for how kind he'd always been to me, and I suggested an expensive and tastelessly fashionable restaurant downtown and said it would be my treat. He again said, No.

I hadn't thought this would be the game he'd play.

"I have something of Ilan's," I finally admitted.

"Good for you," he said, his voice betraying nothing but a cold.

"I mean work. Equations. And what look like billiard ball diagrams. I really don't know what it is. But, well, I had a feeling that you might." I didn't know what I should conceal, but it seemed like I should conceal something. "Maybe it will be important."

"Does it smell like Ilan?"

"I think you should see it."

"Listen, I'll have lunch with you, if that's going to make you happy, but don't be so pathetic as to start thinking you've found some scrap of genius. You should know that Ilan found your interest in him laughable and that his real talent was for convincing people that he was smarter than he was. Which is quite a talent, I won't deny it. But other than that, the only smart ideas that came out of his mouth he stole from other people, usually from me, which is why most everyone, although obviously not you, preferred me—"

Having a "real" life seemed to have worn on Jacob.

At the appointed time and place, Ilan's scrawl in hand, I waited and waited for him. I ordered several courses but ate only a little side of salty cucumbers. Jacob never showed. Maybe he hadn't been the source of the letter. Or maybe he'd lost the spirit to follow through on his joke, whatever it was.

.

A little detective work on my part revealed that Ilan's diagrams had something to do with an idea often played with in science fiction, a problem of causality and time travel known as the grandfather paradox. Simply stated, the paradox is this: if travel to the past is possible—and much in physics suggests that it is—then what happens if you travel back in time and set out to murder your grandfather? If you succeed, then you will never be born, and therefore you won't murder your grandfather, so therefore you will be born, and will be able to murder him, et cetera, ad paradox. Ilan's billiard ball diagrams were part of a tradition (the seminal work is Feynman and Wheeler's 1949 Advanced Absorber Theory) of mathematically analyzing a simplified version of the paradox: imagine a billiard ball enters a wormhole, and then emerges five minutes in the past, on track to hit its earlier self out of the path that sent it into the wormhole in the first place. The surprise is that just as real circles can't be squared, and real moving matter doesn't cross the barrier of the speed of light, the mathematical solutions to the billiard ball–wormhole scenario seem to bear out the notion that real solutions don't generate grandfather paradoxes. The rub is that some of the solutions are exceptionally strange and involve the balls behaving in extraordinarily unlikely, but not impossible, ways. The ball may quantum tunnel, or break in half, or hit up against its earlier self at just such an angle so as to enter the wormhole in just such a way that even more unlikely events occur. But the ball won't, and can't, hit up against its past self in any way that would conflict with its present self's trajectory. The mathematics simply don't allow it. Thus no paradox. Science fiction writers have arrived at analogous solutions to the grandfather paradox: murderous grandchildren are inevitably stopped by something—faulty pistols, slippery banana peels, their own consciences—before the impossible deed can be carried out.

Frankly, I was surprised that Ilan—if it was Ilan—was any good at math. He hadn't seemed the type.

Maybe I was also surprised that I spent so many days trying to understand that note. I had other things to do. Laundry. Work. I was auditing an extra course in Materials. I can't pretend I didn't harbor the hope that eventually—on my own—I'd prove that page some sort of important discovery. I don't know how literally I thought this would bring Ilan back to me. But the image that came to me was that of digging up a grave.

I kind of wanted to call Jacob just to say that he hadn't hurt my feelings by standing me up, that I didn't need his help, or his company, or anything.

.

Time passed. Then one Thursday—it was August—I came across two (searingly dismissive) reviews of a book Jacob had written called *Times and Misdemeanors*. I was amazed that he had completed anything at all. And frustrated that "grandfather paradox" didn't appear in the index. It seemed to me implied by the title, even though that meant reading the title wrongly, as literature. Though obviously the title invited that kind of "wrongness." Which I thought was annoying and ambiguous in precisely a Jacob kind of way. I bought the book, but in some small attempt at dignity, I didn't read it.

The following Monday, for the first time in his life, Jacob called me up. He said he was hoping to discuss something rather delicate with me, something he'd rather not mention over the phone. "What is it?" I asked.

"Can you meet me?" he asked.

"But what is it?"

"What time should we meet?"

I refused the first three meeting times he proposed, because I could. Eventually Jacob suggested we meet at the Moroccan place at whatever time I wanted, that day or the next, but urgently, not farther in the future, please.

"You mean the place where I first met Ilan?" This just slipped out.

"And me. Yes. There."

In preparation for our meeting, I reread the negative reviews of Jacob's book.

And I felt so happy.

·

Predictably, the coffee shop was the same but somehow not quite the same. Someone, not me, was reading the *New York Post*. Someone, not Ilan, was reading Deleuze. The fashion had made for shorter shorts on many of the women, and my lemonade came with slushy, rather than cubed, ice. But the chairs were still trimmed with chipping red paint, and the floor tile seemed, as ever, to fall just short of exhibiting a regular pattern. Jacob walked in only a few minutes late, his gaze detained by one after another set of bare legs. With an expression like someone sucking on an unpleasant cough drop, he made his way over to me.

I offered my sincerest consolations on the poor reviews of his work.

"Oh, time will tell," he said. He looked uncomfortable; he didn't even touch the green leaf cookies I'd ordered for him. Sighing, wrapping his hand tightly around the edge of the table and looking away, he said, "You know what Augustine says about time? Augustine describes time as a symptom

of the world being out of order, a symptom of things in the
world not being themselves, having to make their way back to
themselves, by moving through time—"

Somehow I had already ceded control of the conversation.
No billiard ball diagrams. No Ilan. No reviews. Almost as if
I weren't there, Jacob went on with his unencouraged rumina-
tions: "There's a paradox there, of course, since what can
things be but themselves? In Augustine's view, we live in what
he calls the region of unlikeness, and what we're unlike is God.
We are apart from God, who is pure being, who is himself,
who is outside of time. Time is our tragedy, the substance we
have to wade through as we try to move closer to God. Rivers
flowing to the sea, a flame reaching upward, a bird homing:
these movements are things yearning to reach their true state.
As humans, our motion reflects our yearning for God, and everything we do through time comes from moving, or at least
trying to move, toward God. So that we can be"—someone at a
nearby table cleared his throat judgmentally, which made me
think of Ilan's also being there—"our true selves. So there's a
paradox there again, that we must submit to God, which feels
deceptively like *not* being ourselves, in order to become ourselves. We might call this yearning love, and it's just that we
often mistake *what* we love. We think we love sensuality. Or
admiration. Or, say, another person. But loving another person is just a confusion, an error. Even if it is the kind of error
that a nice, reasonable person might make—"

It struck me that Jacob might be manically depressed and
that in addition to his career, his marriage might not be going
so well, either.

"I mean," Jacob amended, "it's all bullshit, of course, but
aren't I a great guy? Isn't talking to me great? I can tell you
about time and you learn all about Western civilization. Augustine's ideas are beautiful, no? I love this thought that mo-

tion is *about* something, that things have a place to get to, and a person has something to become, and that thing she must become is herself. Isn't that nice?"

Jacob had never sounded more like Ilan. It was getting on my nerves. Maybe Jacob could read my very heart and was trying to insult, or cure, me. "You've never called me before," I said. "I have a lot of work to do, you know."

"Nonsense," he said, without making it clear which statement of mine he was dismissing.

"You said that you wanted to discuss something 'delicate.' "

Jacob returned to the topic of Augustine; I returned to the question of why the two of us had come to sit together right then, right there. We ping-ponged in this way, until eventually Jacob said, "Well, it's about Ilan, so you'll like that."

"About the grandfather paradox?" I said, too quickly.

"Or it could be called the father paradox. Or even the mother paradox."

"I guess I've never thought of it that way, but sure." My happiness had dissipated; I felt angry and manipulated.

"Not only about Ilan but about my work as well." Jacob then began to whisper. "The thing is, I'm going to ask you to try to kill me. Don't worry, I can assure you that you won't succeed. But in attempting, you'll prove a glorious, shunned truth that touches on the nature of time, free will, causal loops, and quantum theory. You'll also probably work out some aggression you feel toward me."

Truth be told, through the thin haze of my disdain, I had always been envious of Jacob's intellect; I had privately believed—despite what those reviews said, or maybe partly because of what those reviews said—that Jacob was a rare genius. Now I realized that he was just crazy.

"I know what you're thinking," Jacob said. "Unfortu-

nately, I can't explain everything to you right here, right now.
It's too psychologically trying. For you, I mean. Listen, come
over to my apartment on Saturday. My family will be away for
the weekend, and I'll explain everything to you then. Don't be
alarmed. You probably know that I've lost my job"—I hadn't
known that, but I should have been able to guess it—"but
those morons, trust me, their falseness will become obvious.
They'll be flies at the horse's ass. My ideas will bestride the
world like a colossus. And you, too: you'll be essential."

I promised to attend, fully intending not to.

"Please," he said.

"Of course," I said.

All the rest of that week I tried to think through my decision carefully, but the more I tried to organize my thoughts,
the more ludicrous I felt for thinking them at all. I thought:
As a friend, isn't it my responsibility to find out if Jacob has
gone crazy? But really we're not friends. And if I come to
know too much about his madness, he may destroy me in order to preserve his psychotic worldview. But maybe I should
take that risk because in drawing closer to Jacob—mad or
not—I'll learn something more of Ilan. But why do I need to
know anything? And do my propositions really follow one
from the other? Maybe my *not going* will entail Jacob's having to destroy me in order to preserve his worldview. Or maybe
Jacob is utterly levelheaded and just bored enough to play an
elaborate joke on me. Or maybe, despite there never having
been the least spark of sexual attraction between us, despite
the fact that we could have been locked in a closet for seven
hours and nothing would have happened, maybe, for some
reason, Jacob is trying to seduce me. Out of nostalgia for Ilan.
Or as consolation for the turn in his career. Was I really up for
dealing with a desperate man?

Or was I, in my dusty way, passing up the opportunity to

be part of an idea that would, as Jacob had said, "bestride the
world like a colossus"?

.

Early Saturday morning I found myself knocking on Jacob's
half-open door; this was when my world began to grow strange
to me—strange and yet also familiar, as if my destiny had
once been known to me and I had forgotten it incompletely.
Jacob's voice invited me in.

I'd never been to his apartment before. It was tiny, and
smelled of orange rinds, and had, incongruously, behind a
futon, a chalkboard; also so many piles of papers and books
that the apartment seemed more like the movie set for an
intellectual's rooms than like the real McCoy. I had once visited a ninety-one-year-old great-uncle who was still conduct-
ing research on fruit flies, and his apartment was cluttered
with countless hand-stoppered jars of cloned fruit flies and
also hot plates for preparing some sort of agar; that apartment was what Jacob's brought to mind. I found myself
doubting that Jacob truly had a wife and child, as he had so
often claimed.

"Thank God you've come," Jacob said, emerging from
what appeared to be a galley kitchen but may have been simply
a closet. "I knew you'd be reliable, that at least." And then, as
if reading my mind: "Natasha sleeps in the loft we built. My
wife and I sleep on the futon. Although yes, it's not much for
entertaining. But can I get you something? I have this tea that
one of my students gave me, exceptional stuff from Japan,
harvested at high altitude—"

"Tea, great, yes," I said. To my surprise, I was relieved that
Jacob's ego seemed to weather his miserable surroundings just
fine. Also to my surprise I felt tenderly toward him. And toward the scent of old citrus.

On the main table I noticed what looked like the ragtag remains of some Physics 101 lab experiments: rusted silver balls on different inclines, distressed balloons, a stained funnel, a markered flask, a calcium-speckled Bunsen burner, iron filings and sandpaper, large magnets, and yellow batteries likely bought from a Chinese immigrant on the subway. Did I have the vague feeling that "a strange traveler" might show up and tell "extravagant stories" over a meal of fresh rabbit? I did. I also considered that Jacob's asking me to murder him had just been an old-fashioned suicidal plea for help.

"Here, here." Jacob brought me tea in a cracked porcelain cup.

I thought, somewhat fondly, of Ilan's old inscrutable poisoning jokes. "Thanks so much," I said. I moved away from that table of hodgepodge and sat on Jacob's futon.

"Well," Jacob said gently, also sitting down.

"Yes, well."

"Well, well."

"Yes," I said.

"I'm not going to hit on you," Jacob said.

"Of course not. You're not going to kiss my hand."

"No."

The tea tasted like damp cotton.

Jacob rose and walked over to the table, spoke to me from across the compressed distance. "I presume that you learned what you could. From those scribblings of Ilan. Yes?"

I conceded. Both that I had learned something and that I had not learned everything. That much was still a mystery to me.

"But you understand, at least, that in situations approaching grandfather paradoxes very strange things can become the norm. Just as if someone running begins to approach the speed of light, he grows unfathomably heavy." He paused.

"Didn't you find it odd that you found yourself lounging so much with me and Ilan? Didn't it seem to beg explanation, how happy the three of us—"

"It wasn't strange," I insisted. I was right almost by definition. It wasn't strange because it had already happened and so it was conceivable. Or maybe that was wrong. "I think he loved us both," I said, confused for no reason. "And we both loved him."

Jacob sighed. "Yes, OK. I hope you'll appreciate the elaborate calculations I've done in order to set up these demonstrations of extraordinarily unlikely events. Come over here. Please. You'll see that we're in a region of, well, not exactly a region of unlikeness, that would be a cheap association—very Ilan-like, though, a fitting tribute—but we'll enter a region where things seem not to behave as themselves. In other words, a zone where events, teetering toward interfering"—I briefly felt that I was a child again, falling asleep on our scratchy blue sofa while my coughing father watched reruns of *Twilight Zone*—"with a fixed future, are pressured into revealing their hidden essences."

I felt years or miles away.

Then this happened, which is not the crux of the story, or even the center of what was strange to me: Jacob tapped one of the silver balls and it rolled up the inclined plane; he set a flask of water on the Bunsen burner and marked the rising level of the fluid; a balloon distended unevenly; a magnet under sandpaper moved iron filings so as to spell the word "egregious."

Jacob turned to me, raised his eyebrows. "Astonishing, no?"

I felt like I'd seen him wearing a dress or going to the bathroom. What he had shown me were children's magic tricks.

"I remember those science magic shows from childhood," I said gently. I wasn't *not* afraid. "I always loved those spooky caves they advertised on highway billboards." Cousin or no cousin, Ilan had clearly run away from Jacob, not from me.

"I can see you're resistant," Jacob said. "Which I understand, and even respect. Maybe I scared you, with that killing me talk, which you weren't ready for. We'll return to it. I'll order us in some food. We'll eat, we'll drink, we'll talk, and I'll let you absorb the news slowly. You're an engineer, for God's sake. You'll put the pieces together. Sometimes sleep helps, sometimes spearmint—just little ways of sharpening a mind's ability to synthesize. You take your time."

.

Jacob transferred greasy Chinese food into marginally clean bowls, "for a more homey feel." There at the table, that shabby impromptu lab, I found myself eating slowly. Jacob seemed to need something from me, something more, even, than just a modicum of belief. He had paid for the takeout. Halfway through a bowl of wide beef-flavored noodles—we had actually been comfortable in the quiet, at ease—Jacob said, "Didn't you find Ilan's ideas uncannily fashionable? Always a nose ahead? Even how he started wearing pink before everyone else?"

"He was fashionable in all sorts of ways," I agreed, surprised by my appetite for the slippery and unpleasant food. "Not that it ever got him very far, always running after the next new thing. Sometimes I'd copy what he said, and it would sound dumb coming out of my mouth, so maybe it was dumb in the first place. Just said with charm." Never before had I spoken aloud anything unkind about Ilan.

"You don't understand," Jacob said. "I guess I should tell you that Ilan is my as yet unborn son, who visited me—us—from the future." He took a metal ball between two greasy fingers, dropped it twice, and then once again demonstrated it rolling up the inclined plane. "The two of us, Ilan and I, we collaborate." Jacob explained that part of what Ilan had established in his travels, which were repeated and varied, was that contrary to popular movies, travel into the past didn't alter the future, or, rather, that the future was already altered, or, rather, that it was all far more complicated than that. "I, too, was reluctant to believe," Jacob insisted. "Extremely reluctant. And he's my son. A pain in the ass, but also my beloved child." Jacob ate a dumpling in one bite. "A bit too much of a moralist, though. Not a good business partner, in that sense."

I no longer felt intimidated by Jacob. How could I? He had looped the loop. "If Ilan was from the future, that means he could tell you about your future," I said.

"Sure, yes. A little." Jacob blushed like a schoolgirl. "It's not important. But certain things he did know. Yes. Being my son and all."

"Ah, so." I, too, ate a dumpling whole. Which isn't the kind of thing I normally do. "What about my future? Did he know anything about my future?"

Jacob shook his head. I couldn't tell if he was answering my question or just disapproving of it. "Right now we have my career to save," he said. I saw that he was sweating, even along his exposed collarbone. "Can I tell you what I'm thinking? What I'm thinking is that we *perform* the impossibility of my dying before fathering Ilan. A little stunt show of sorts, but for real. With real guns and rope and poison and maybe some blindfolded throwing of knives. Real life. And this can drum up a bit of publicity for my work." I felt myself getting sleepy during this speech of his, getting sleepy and thinking of circuses and of childhood trips to Las Vegas and of Ilan's mattress and of the time a small binder clip landed on my head when I was walking outside. "I mean, it's a bit lowbrow, but lowbrow is the new highbrow, of course, or maybe the old highbrow. It'll be fantastic. Maybe we can go on *Letterman*. I bet we'll make loads of money in addition to getting me my job back. Let's be careful, though. Just because I can't die doesn't mean I can't be pretty seriously injured. But I've been doing some calculations and we've got some real showstoppers—"

"I'm not much of a showgirl," I said, suppressing a yawn. "You can find someone better than me for the job."

Jacob looked at me intently. "We're meant to have this future together," he said. "My wife—she really will want to kill me when she finds out the situation I'm in. She won't cooperate."

"I know people who can help you, Jacob," I said, in the monotone of the half-asleep. "But I can't help you. I like you, though. I really do."

"What's wrong with you? Have you ever seen a marble roll *up* like that? I mean, these are just little anomalies, I didn't want to frighten you, but there are many others. Right here in this room even. We have the symptoms of leaning up against time here."

I thought of Jacob's blathering on about Augustine and meaningful motion and yearning. I also felt convinced I'd been drugged. Not just because of my fatigue but because I was beginning to find Jacob vaguely attractive. His sweaty collarbone was pretty. The room around me—the futon, the Chinese food, the porcelain teacup, the rusty laboratory, the piles of papers, Ilan's note in my back pocket, Jacob's cheap dress socks, the dust, Jacob's ringed hand on his knee—these all seemed like players in a life of mine that had not yet become real, a life I was coursing toward. "Do you think," I found myself asking, maybe because I'd had this feeling just once before in my life, "that Ilan was a rare and tragic genius?"

Jacob laughed.

I shrugged. I leaned my sleepy head against his shoulder. I put my hand to his collarbone.

"I can tell you this about your future," Jacob said quietly. "I didn't not hear that question. So let me soothsay this. You'll never get over Ilan. And that will one day horrify you. But soon enough you'll settle on a replacement object for all that love of yours, which does you about as much good as a life jacket in a train wreck. Your present, if you'll excuse my saying so, is a pretty sorry one. But your future looks great. Your work will amount to nothing. But you'll have a brilliant child. And a brilliant husband. And great love."

He was saying we would be together. He was saying we would be in love. I understood. I had solved the puzzle. I knew who I, who we were meant to be.

.

I woke up alone on Jacob's futon. At first I couldn't locate Jacob, but then I saw he was sleeping in his daughter's loft. His mouth was open; he looked awful. The room smelled of MSG. I felt at once furious and small. I left the apartment, vowing never to go to the coffee shop—or anywhere else I might see Jacob—again. I spent my day grading student exams. That evening I went to the video store and almost rented *Wuthering Heights,* then switched to *The Man Who Wasn't There,* then, feeling haunted in a dumb way, ended up renting nothing at all.

Did I, in the following weeks and months, think of Jacob often? Did I worry for or care about him? I couldn't tell if I did or didn't. Can I even say I'm sure that Jacob was delusional? When King Laius abandons baby Oedipus in the mountains, from fear of the prophecy that his son will murder him, Laius's attempt to evade his destiny becomes its engine. They call this a predestination paradox. It's a variant of the grandfather paradox. At its heart is inescapable fate.

The general theory of relativity is compatible with the existence of space-times in which travel to the past or remote future is possible; we are told by those who would know that the logician Kurt Gödel proved this in the late 1940s. But whether or not a person, in our very particular space-time, can in fact travel to the past—no one knows. Maybe. Surely our world obeys rules still alien to our imaginations. Maybe Jacob is my destiny. Regardless, I continue to avoid him.

STICKER SHOCK

Gross income for the daughter in 2007 was $18,150. Gross income for the mother in 2007 was $68,742. Gross income for the daughter in 2008 was $23,450; in 2009, it was $232,476; in 2010, $140,702; and in 2011, $37,853. The mother's gross income for the years 2008 to 2011 inclusive has not been ascertained. But it is believed to have been, in each of those years, not more than $99,999 and not less than $40,000. Income averaging has not been allowed under the federal tax code since 1986.

From 2007 to 2011, the daughter put $170,000 into savings: $25,000 went into a SEP-IRA, $9,000 went into a Roth IRA, and the remainder was placed in a money market fund. Other money went, as the mother might put it, into the hands of petty charlatans who didn't make it into law or medical school and whose parents, with their values, never taught them anything, poor things, actually, poor things. Or it went, as others might put it, into the hands of venders of artisanal chocolates and $90 T-shirts.

In 1997, while the mother was employed as a technical consultant at a corporation then of good financial standing—though it should be noted that within seven years the corporation then of good financial standing had downsized to 32 percent of its 1997 size and the mother was among those who had not retained their positions, and though she had received a variety of severance package, it was not a variety worth describing and so it will not be described, and the option that the mother had thought she had to retain her health insurance at the same corporate rate had, despite many phone calls, not materialized; instead, the rate offered was more than three times what it had been previously. To return: While holding this position, in which she was consistently earning upward of $90,000 per year, plus respectable benefits, the mother made a down payment of $65,000 toward the purchase of a modest one-bedroom apartment in a condominium building in good standing on the far but not too far east side of Manhattan's Upper East Side. Fungibility precludes saying where the money for the down payment came from—whether from contemporary earnings or from preexisting savings. It was what it was. Money was spent. Or, rather, was converted into an asset.

The mother purchased the apartment not for herself but for her daughter. It was not intended, however, that the daughter live in the apartment. The daughter did not live in, or even very near, the city of New York. The apartment was, rather, an investment gift. An informal living trust. Both the mother's and the daughter's names were put on the mortgage. Both the mother's and the daughter's names were put on the title. The daughter was specified as 99 percent owner, and the mother was specified as 1 percent owner. This arrangement was superior for tax purposes and in the case of unexpected death. The mother intended that the asset/apartment could be rented for a sum that would cover the combined mortgage and maintenance payments, and this, more or less, happened.

Although not really: the asset/apartment was "rented" for free to the mother's son—the daughter's brother—until such time as he and his new and approved-of and soon-to-be-pregnant wife felt more financially stable. During this time of intrafamilial "renting," the mother covered the monthly mortgage and maintenance payments herself. A substantial portion of the mortgage payment, being interest rather than principal, was tax deductible, she (the mother) notes. So it wasn't really such a draining gift, the mother says. The reason the mother had purchased the asset/apartment in behalf of her daughter, as opposed to in behalf of her wed and soon-to-procreate son, was that the mother had, a number of years earlier, made an investment of similar size in behalf of her son, and so the mother felt that this second gift, to her second offspring, was only fair. The first offspring would live there, but the asset part of the asset/apartment would all the while offer a measure of financial security to the second offspring. It is true that, in general, the mother greatly preferred men to women—the daughter similarly greatly preferred men to women—but the mother nevertheless, most likely, loved her children equally, inasmuch as it is not nonsensical to make equating statements about nonfungibles such as love.

One was trying to account for things. To appreciate was to estimate justly.

Regarding the relations between men and women generally, the mother had, early and often, instructed the daughter that: A Woman Should Always Be Financially Independent. On the point of financial independence, the daughter agreed with the mother. And still agrees. However, the daughter's accord with the postulate, which was during childhood like a faith in the gnostic cult of numbers of Pythagoras, later became a variety of realpolitik. (The mother's realpolitik outlook was like a faith in a gnostic cult of numbers.) Regardless of any kind of regarding of the relations among men, women, and finance, the aforementioned asset/apartment, between 1998 and 2006, appreciated in value by approximately $512,000. It was then sold, which left, after all expenses, kind of a lot of money. All of which was put into a bank account somewhere. The daughter did not know where. The mother did. Later this led to a dispute.

·

In 1994, the daughter had moved from the family home to a dorm room at a sufficiently prestigious university. The usual education loans were applied for, approved, and taken. The loans were taken under the daughter's name. The daughter held a number of on-campus jobs. The daughter was relatively frugal in those years. But it would be fair to say that the mother paid for most everything. Also in 1994, the mother was widowed, to the gain of no pension or Social Security; the non-gain was due to technical problems, problems that probably could have been overcome, but there was just so much to do, it seemed.

During the first year of mother-daughter residential separation, a year that also witnessed the trial of O. J. Simpson, the mother mailed the daughter various photographs of the prosecutor Marcia Clark. The mother greatly admired Marcia Clark's outfits. She hoped the trial lawyer's style might positively influence, perhaps even inspire, the daughter, who did not dress like Marcia Clark, and who did not seem to be on track to becoming anything like Marcia Clark. The daughter did not appear to be en route to becoming any variety of Financially Independent Woman with which the mother was familiar. One might even say—one being alternately the mother and the daughter—that this was the mother's fault: the mother had packed so many lunches, had paid for so many lessons, had so often put towels and clean clothes in the dryer for five minutes so they'd be warm for the daughter after a bath, that she, the daughter, had understandably developed a misimpression of what life was like. Now the daughter needed guidance. At the end of 1995, the mother moved to the same town to which the daughter had moved. Also at the end of 1995, the daughter began a relationship with a young man; after that relationship had begun, the daughter's ability to register anything about any situation save the young man's presence or absence in it declined precipitately. The daughter and the young man later married. The mother said she was glad for this. This was one of the few decisions made by the daughter of which the mother approved. The mother paid for the wedding.

In the spring of 2010, the daughter and the man broke up. The reasons for the marriage's end are not clear, though there are theories. The main cause of the rapid appreciation in the value of real estate in that time has also not been satisfactorily determined, though there are, again, theories; one, again, tries to account for things. Regardless, the daughter wanted to use the money from the sale of the asset/apartment to buy herself an apartment/asset—an apartment/asset to live in as a home. The mother did not agree with or to this. The mother would not specify the location of what had previously been described as the daughter's money, because the daughter was "not the daughter that I know because the daughter that I know is not a cruel person," the mother said. She further said that the current daughter, the unknown one, could not be trusted, not with her own money, not with her own reproductive potential, not with anything, really. The daughter needed to go back home. To her husband's apartment. To where she belonged. Whatever unhappiness and fears were keeping the couple apart were pure childishness. The mother said that the daughter had always done exactly as she (the daughter) wanted, that the daughter was lazy, and that women who don't have babies become alcoholics, which ruins their figures. The daughter was thirty-three.

In 2010, the mother was in some ways financially stable and in some ways not. (It depends, of course, on the comparison group.) The mother often reported that she did not *feel* financially stable. The mother also was often trying to lose weight. Sometimes the two anxieties, weight and money, joined

together. For example, in the fall of 2010, the mother signed
up with the Jenny Craig Weight Loss program. The program
entailed paying in advance for prepared meals. On Wednesdays, when she went to the Jenny Craig Centre [*sic*] for her
appointment with her Jenny Consultant—the consultant being another service that she paid for in advance—the mother
picked up the prepaid meals. In addition to the meal and the
consultant expenses, the mother also, at the Jenny Craig Centre, purchased, for $190, a specialized armband, enabled with
Bluetooth wireless technology, that kept track of walking
speed, heart rate, calories burned, calories in and out, meta-
bolic something-or-other . . . it was all confusing. The armband was supposed to be able to monitor and communicate.
Sometimes the armband seemed to know she was moving and
sometimes it didn't. It beeped unpredictably. Also it flashed.
For a few days the armband would not light up at all. Then it
unexpectedly revived. Then it alarmed hourly. The armband
was a failure; the mother wanted a refund. But, as the mother
explained to her daughter, the Jenny Consultant said that,
while it was true that Jenny Craig did sell the armband on-site
at the Centre, and that the consultant and the program did
both believe that the armband could be a positive friend in
any weight loss or weight maintenance regimen, still, the armband was not a Jenny Craig armband per se, and the Jenny
Craig Centre did not represent the armband, or the armband
makers, nor did the armband or its makers represent the
Jenny Craig Centre, and the Jenny Craig Centre did not even
formally endorse the armband's makers, or vice versa—there
was no real relation—and so the mother needed to address
her inquiries or complaints *not* to the Jenny Craig Centre but
to the armband company directly. Whose number the Jenny
Consultant would be happy to look up for her. The mother
called the company directly. Her calls were not returned. The
daughter also rarely returned the mother's calls. The mother

e-mailed the company. The mother and the daughter arranged via e-mail to meet up for coffee, and it was during that coffee that the mother explained that three days after e-mailing the armband company, she received an e-mail response: a FAQ sheet with the phone number she had already called listed at the bottom, for any further questions. Eventually, the mother said, she got through on the phone to someone who represented the company that represented the armband that was failing her. This representative suggested that the mother return the armband, in its original packaging. The representative further specified that the armband would, if it showed no signs of wear and tear beyond that incurred in normal use, be serviced and returned to the mother within four to six weeks. Are you just trying to stall until you can get rid of me? the mother said she said to the representative. The mother said she said to the representative that he was representing a company of cheaters. The mother hung up the phone, she said. Later that day, the mother explained to the daughter, she told the Jenny Consultant that the armband company had not helped, of course, that she had been encouraged to buy an armband from a charlatan company, that she had been encouraged by these people right here, in this office, these Jenny Craig people, who, the mother said that she said to the Jenny Consultant, obviously didn't care about their customers, who didn't have an ethic of customer service, who were just squeezing people for money. The mother said she said, You took my hundred and ninety dollars for what you knew was junk and now you're just sending me to hell. You know that's where you're sending me when you send me to contact the company directly. I work in service. I like working in service. I like to help people. I know what an ethic of customer service is, the mother said, and it isn't this. (The mother, at the time, post-corporate-job, was working as a real estate broker in the city; the real estate market was considerably weaker than it had been during the years of the aforementioned rise in value of the asset/apartment.) The mother said to the daughter that she really shouted at them, the Jenny Craig people, that she felt a little bit bad about that, but that what they did was wrong and they should know that what they did was wrong. But, she explained to the daughter, she did not need the Jenny Craig program anymore. She did not need them. Though she had lost ten pounds since she started with the program. Could the daughter tell? It's not the first ten pounds, the mother explained, that anyone notices. It would probably be the *next* ten pounds that people would be able to notice, the next ten, which would of course be more difficult to lose, but she now knew what Jenny Craig did and so she could do it without Jenny Craig. She had cracked it. You eat twelve hundred calories a day. You make sure to get twenty grams of protein. Your meals are around three hundred and fifty calories, and then there's room for two fruits. She said, I'm doing it like this: I'm making lentil dishes that are high in protein and low in calories. For example, I made a vegetarian chopped liver dip. One cup dry lentils, two cups water, one tablespoon onion soup powder, two large stir-fried onions, two hard-boiled eggs—all blended together. It's delicious. You should try it, the mother said. That's what I wanted to tell you about.

The daughter said she thought that sounded good.

Then they were quiet for a bit. Then the mother began to talk about how a friend of hers had cervical cancer; she'd never had children, the mother explained of her friend; it's a risk to one's health to never have children. I pray to God that you will have a child. You are a difficult person, but you can get pregnant, you can even just go to a clinic these days and get pregnant. There's nothing wrong with that. The daughter put some sugar in her coffee, even though she almost never put sugar in her coffee. The mother reminded the daughter of the story of the cousin who had gotten pregnant, most likely from a clinic, the cousin who people said was a lesbian but, the mother said, was probably just never lucky with men, but it didn't matter, because the cousin was so happy now, even though she had always been a very ill-tempered person before, and the mother said that she (the mother) would pay any medical expenses there might be, that she would help the daughter.

The daughter didn't respond.

The mother told the daughter that it was interesting that she (the daughter) had chosen that day to wear a green shirt and green shorts, all green like that, together. The mother reiterated that the daughter really should try making the vegetarian chopped liver dip. Which is low in calories while being very tasty. The daughter said, All you care about is money and weight; and you give me all this advice; but I'm thinner than you and I make more money than you.

The daughter had been rejected for a mortgage earlier that day; or, rather, she had not been rejected, but she had been approved for a mortgage of only thirty-five thousand dollars. Which was grossly insufficient. The rejection stemmed partly from the daughter's unstable income—her income was unstable because she had not followed the mother's career advice—and partly from recent crises in the mortgage industry, which had led to the lender's not accepting 1099 income in the same way as W-2 income. Now the apartment/asset was absolutely unbuyable without the mother's help.

The mother restated that the daughter should go back to her husband. The mother wanted to help the couple buy a nice place to live. A place that would also be a nice investment property, a condominium that they could rent out when they needed a new and larger place to live, because of children. Yes, the purchase should be of a condominium and not of a cooperative, though the mother acknowledged that the daughter *said* that she tended not to like the newer condominium buildings, but she knew that the daughter just felt pressure to express that taste—for older buildings—which was not in fact really her taste. She was just being forced into that taste by trends that would pass, just as this rough spot in the marriage would pass. If they, the daughter and her husband, had a nice place to live, then they would find happiness, because it's hard to find happiness when you don't have space to breathe and she wanted her daughter to breathe.

You were very right, the daughter said, when you used to tell me that A Woman Should Always Be Financially Independent.

I didn't think you ever listened to me. I'm honored, the mother said.

The daughter said to the mother that the money that was gifted to her by her mother was really the mother's money and not hers, it was true. But she felt that the money should either be her money or not be her money, and that she could not tolerate any in-betweens and she could not tolerate any health or fashion advice, either—that was it. The mother said she wasn't giving advice, just love. The daughter left. The mother paid the bill.

.

In February 2011, the mother and the daughter made a plan to meet again for coffee. It had been many months of meetings "for coffee" and very little accord. The mother had said that she would bring the checkbook for the account where the profits from the asset/apartment were kept. The daughter showed up to the meeting.

What do you think "homey" means? the mother asked.

Why are you asking me that? the daughter asked.

You're so suspicious, the mother said. You think the worst of me. I give up, the mother said. Then she said, It's just something that was on my mind because of a client I had. A while ago. He was Swedish. He was looking to buy a studio in New York, because he couldn't handle the Swedish winter anymore and so he wanted to winter in New York. Which sounds odd, to winter in New York, but that's what he said, that he just needed a place to lay his head, and that it could be tiny, it just needed to have lots of natural light. I understood him, the mother said. He also said he liked New York because it's inexpensive, which sounded funny to me, like the wintering, but that was what he said, that New York was cheap. So I took him to a beautiful studio with windows on three sides. Not just ordinary windows but really tall ones, and the apartment was clean and beautiful with good appliances and a gorgeous floor and, like I said, so much light; it was really such a good value, and I thought that I myself would be happy to live there, and I was so happy with what I was showing him. He only stayed for a minute, though. I can't live here, he said. It doesn't feel homey. That was the word he used: "homey." I thanked the listing broker, and then when we were back outside, I said to the Swede—I liked the guy, so I was honest with him—I said, You don't know how fortunate you are to see a place like this in Manhattan. It's a tremendous value. I'm just telling you, because you'll see other places, and they won't be as nice, and I don't want you to be disappointed. I'm not, he said, going to buy a place until I find exactly what I want. What you'll learn, I said, is that this is the city of compromises. I'm not talking about you, the mother said to the daughter. I know you think I am, but I'm not. I wanted to tell you about the second apartment I showed the Swede. When I showed him another place, he brought a friend with him. You should have seen his friend. He had this very long, very black hair. And pale, pale skin. He looked like a man you see in advertisements for cigarettes, or speedboats. I mean, he looked like a racecar driver. And he *was* a racecar driver! This is my friend, the Swede said to me, the mother said. He just got back from a racecar competition in Abu Dhabi, the Swede explained. So I mentioned that you had been to Abu Dhabi.

I haven't been to Abu Dhabi, the daughter said.

I thought you had.

No.

Oh.

I was in Dubai, though.

I thought they were the same.

No.

I said to the racecar driver that I had heard that Abu Dhabi was a ghost town, with all those vacant apartments.

That's Dubai, the daughter said.

Oh. It's Dubai that has a lot of empty apartment buildings?

Right. Abu Dhabi is supposedly doing pretty well.

You probably think the Swede and his friend didn't like me, but they liked me very much, the mother said. Many people like me. They feel good around me. I took the Swede and his dramatic friend to an apartment on Park Avenue and Thirty-ninth Street. In one of those grand old buildings. Where many people who used to have live-in maids no longer have live-in maids, and so there are these small apartments that used to be maids' apartments. I thought the Swede might like it. But as soon as I walked into the apartment I felt awful for taking the Swede there. I hadn't had a chance to preview it. It had looked much better in the pictures. There was just one window, and it was in the corner and was tiny. The place had terrible old furniture, there was an ugly cat there, the floor had rotting parquet. The Swede took a quick walk around; he looked at his racecar driver friend. Now *this* feels homey, he said. His friend nodded. I was amazed. What does he mean that it feels homey?

It was like a puzzle. It stuck with me. It made me think that maybe I'm really missing something, that maybe if I better understood what he meant, then maybe I would be doing better.

I bet he just likes old buildings, the daughter said. I like old buildings.

But it was disgusting, the mother said.

Or maybe it was just that it had furniture. Just that someone lived there.

I thought about that. And, you know, later the broker from the first apartment called me and asked me for feedback. She asked me what my client thought. I told her honestly that he hadn't liked it. But I told her, also honestly, that I thought it was beautiful, and that it was crazy of him not to like it. She asked me what he didn't like about it, because she was trying to think how she could better market the apartment, because she was having, she said, to be honest, trouble selling it, even though she felt it was well priced. I felt bad for her. She sounded distressed. I told her it's hard to sell anything right now, even something great. I told her not to worry, that things would turn around.

Did the Swede buy the maid's apartment? the daughter asked.

Oh, in the end, he didn't buy anything from me, the mother said. He liked me, though. He said I was honest. He didn't buy anything at all. Instead, he moved to Dubai.

What?

He moved to Dubai instead of New York.

To Dubai? Or to Abu Dhabi?

I don't know. Somewhere sunny.

That's too bad, the daughter said. I think. About the apartment, I mean. But you have to stop confusing things. That's why you come to the wrong conclusions. Because you start in the wrong place. So then you're not really even talking about what you're talking about, the daughter went on, not really sure what she herself was talking about, and realizing that she had lost track of precisely what it was that she was trying to estimate justly, and why she had imagined that she could.

AMERICAN INNOVATIONS

This was in Singapore City, midday in an August. I was visiting my thin, tan, sixty-something non-native-of-Singapore aunt of exceptional math skills who had made her fortune, from near enough to nothing, in spandex and sequin fashions. When I was younger, we had called her Tina Turner because her styling was similar—also, she had once seen Tina Turner in a grocery store in Los Angeles, and they had nodded knowingly at one another, that was the story—but now my aunt seemed smaller, and tamer, if still disturbingly "hot," considerably more hot than either of her daughters, both now middle-aged and involved in their own relatively less demanding lives, in more prosaic bodies, in other countries. My aunt still shared her mahogany-interiored seven-bedroom house—it was a sixties construction, with lots of obtuse angles, so that you could make right after right after right after right and still not be facing your original direction—with her husband of all those years, although he left for the beach by 5:00 a.m. most days, and she was a night person, and so it was as if she lived alone. After 11:00 p.m., she liked to play bridge online, often with people "in your sorts of time zones." My aunt told me that not everyone in the online bridge world was very nice; in fact, it was difficult to believe how rude some people could be; really, it was amazing.

"This guy, we were partners; he opened a heart, and then

he rebid two spades over my no-trump—that's a reverse. Do
you understand bidding? It's like he was going backward.
Look, it's not common. To do that, you're essentially promising your partner that you have at least sixteen high card
points. At least. Are you following? For him to make that bid,
he's saying he's got long hearts and a really good hand. And
then he doesn't, not at all! We end up in four hearts in a four-
two fit. It's like he's expecting *me* to have the hearts, it's crazy.
Everyone else is in a normal three no-trump. So I write to
him: 'Are you drunk or are you stupid?' "

"You said, 'Are you drunk or are you stupid?' "

"Yes, you can make chatter in the sidebar of the game.
There's a space. I mean, you don't even play bridge, but even
you can understand that he made a ridiculous bid, right? I've
read six books on bridge; you can trust me, what he did was
really idiotic. That's why I said what I said. Well, then he called
me awful names. Just awful. I can't say the names. And he was
the one who made the mistake! I almost didn't want to play
bridge online ever again. And I have some very nice people that
I play bridge with. But I almost gave up playing. See, that's
what happens with the Internet. Some people will be amaz-
ingly rude."

I think I said something about how yes, people could really be people.

She said something about how I must be jet-lagged.

"I'm all right," I said. The main reason I was in Singapore
was that a year-and-a-half-long relationship of mine had recently come to an end, and it had seemed natural to transi-
tion by visiting a friend who had moved to Hong Kong, and
then, already so far, visiting my aunt, too. I wasn't devastated,
though; it wasn't that kind of breakup; my serial eighteen-
month relationships consistently ended amicably, it was just a
weird tic of mine, one with which I was fine. It was like, I had
been told, I wasn't a woman.

"Did I ever tell you," my aunt asked, "about my September 11th?"

No, she hadn't.

"It was late here, everyone was asleep, and my God, I was lying in bed, and then I noticed this lump, quite big, right here, on my side. I was sure it was cancer. I was sure I was going to die. How could I have not noticed it before?" She went on to say, "It was right here at these low ribs that aren't full ribs. Normally I would have called my friend Simona, she's an excellent doctor, you know, but I didn't think it was right, ringing her late like that. That's nighttime thinking for you. I'm sure she wouldn't have minded. But I told myself I would have to make it on my own until the beginning of the next business day. That's what I was thinking. I couldn't rest, of course. I went and turned on the television, just to distract myself, to calm myself down. And what's there? The towers. Can you believe it? I mean, how awful. And they just kept replaying it. I sat there watching it all alone. Well, it wasn't cancer, the lump. It was just my breast. I mean, the silicone. The implant. It just fell down. Unbelievable, right? That they would put something in you that could do that. I said to the doctors, Just take it out and never give it back to me. I like small breasts now. I used to hate them, but now I like them."

"That's awful," I said. "I mean, about how scared you must have been."

Then my Tina asked me, "Are you still working on your physical therapy thing?"

That had been two career interests ago, but it was a thoughtful inquiry, considering that we didn't see each other very often. "Oh," I said. "No."

When we set out to get a bite to eat, I was relieved.

"They have excellent salads at this place," my aunt said. "The best outfit is a good figure."

I agreed.

•

A year and some later, in Chapel Hill, North Carolina, I awoke from not particularly uneasy dreams. I was sleeping alone and on my stomach. It was not September 11th. I negotiated nine more minutes from the alarm. Then the alarm went off again; I negotiated again; then the alarm again, and then, like so many other mornings, I got out of bed.

In the bathroom, I washed my face with peach scrub and took care, as I generally do, not to look into the mirror too *gesamtkunstwerk*-ily. Instead, only in close patches. Only enough to rest reasonably assured that nothing too grotesque has overnight arrived on or departed from my face, and that I have scrubbed away all the applied scrub. It's important to avoid mirrors if one is unprepared to accept their daily news, and I think, in something as insignificantly devastating as appearance, denial is more socially constructive than despondency. Not that there's anything especially wrong with me—just the usual.

However, in the hallway downstairs there's a mirror you see yourself in even when you don't intentionally look.

That mirror claimed there was a substantial lump on the right side of my lower back. An anatomically anomalous and yet familiar-seeming lump.

I would have just looked away but it was like seeing a burn victim or a really beautiful person: I couldn't unstare. My hand moved to the mass. The mass liked being touched. I lifted my shirt. I would say what I saw was a wow. Even though it was modest, maybe a B cup in size. It didn't need support. It manifested all the expected anatomy, the detailing of which I feel is private. What I saw was really textbook. Save for its location, there on my back. As if to hide from me. Or as if to discreetly maintain an unacknowledged child. Though the discreetness would work only in a world in which we meet one another exclusively head-on, or possibly in three-quarters profile. Because in profile the anatomy really could not be denied.

I pulled my shirt back down. It was fitted but, thankfully, long.

Was this an inheritance?

I made myself sunny-side-up eggs. The newspaper informed me that a young volunteer worker at a large-cat reserve had been killed by a lion. Her parents said their daughter had been doing what she loved, there at the reserve; she had never been happier; protocol had been followed; it was a rare and tragic accident and not the result of carelessness; the parents did not blame the reserve; they listed the large-cat sanctuary as one of the charities to which mourners might elect to donate in lieu of flowers. I'm not saying I didn't feel disfigured and humiliated. But I know such things are mainly a matter of mind.

.

Like the girl pounced on and accidentally killed by the large cat, I also was attempting to do something I loved. I was studying Library Sciences. I had always loved libraries. No one looks at you there, and you can look at everyone, so people probably are looking at you, just like you're looking at them, but it's all nice and quiet, and everyone can stay inside his or her headspace. But I hadn't really known what library sciences was, and it turned out to be highly nonoverlapping with what I had deduced from the blurred, squinting assessment I had made of it from a distance with as little information—"information" being a word and concept I both dislike and distrust—as possible. Then it turned out I wasn't even really in a Library Sciences program, I was in a Library *and Information* Sciences program, the core of which focused on

"Humans becoming informed via intermediation between inquirers and instrumented records." I was learning computer skills, basically. I was becoming trained as a searcher of databases. I was taking a metadata course on Indexing and Cataloging and another course on Knowledge Management.

That first day of my supernumeraryness I went to the school library for a timed assignment, done from my pale blue laminated tin carrel. It was a set of twenty query transformations. Query transformations are just what they sound like. A human has a curiosity—something simple, like, What are the seasons like in Mongolia? or less simple, like, How was gender represented in the literature of Heian Japan?—and ideally, the library information scientist will translate that curiosity into intelligently delimited searches in well-chosen databases that then return navigable information.

Whatever. Number twenty-one on the assignment was to generate one's own query and query results. I chose not to query my body's recent developments; even more than mirrors, Internet reflections combine the qualia of unflinching and unfaithful. I had once, via the Internet, tried to learn about the anthropologist Margaret Mead. After an hour I was left only with a strong impression that Mead's primary intellectual contribution had been the adding of an *s* to the term "semiotic." That, and having taken a female lover for much of her later life. I assumed, and continue to assume, that there are more important things to know about Mead, although how would I know?

At noon I attended a lecture given by Professor Sidwell. The lecture was about the problem of acidification—what to do about the hydrolysis of paper in books, the "slow fires" caused by the low pH levels of the paper commonly used for printing during certain key decades. Professor Sidwell had the same sloping posture my dad had had, and so I felt closer to him than in reality I was. Early on in the term, I'd had a conversation with him in the cafeteria in which he said that American cuisine had gone downhill since the 1940s. His grandmother had been a great cook, but she was the last of the Mohicans. I said, Wasn't it at least an improvement to know about Chinese food? About soy sauce? No, he said. It wasn't. Widely available refrigeration? I asked. No, Sidwell answered, refrigeration has been awful. Refrigeration has been absolutely catastrophic.

In the lecture that day Sidwell was saying, among other things, that the new de-acidification processes—there were several of them, and they were all bad—were leaving the treated paper with an unpleasant texture (the wrong texture), depositing powders, sometimes causing colored inks to run, and leaving clamp marks on books' bodies. De-acidification was hastening destruction, not delaying it.

After the lecture I went up to Professor Sidwell, to see if he'd notice my altered self. Also just to say hello. "Ah, the refrigeration advocate," he said. He barely looked at me. "Are things well in the land of the young and innovative?"

"I really liked the lecture," I said. "I guess you're damned if you do and damned if you don't."

"No, no, that's not quite accurate," he said. He looked me over. His tone softened notably as he said, "I don't want you to take this in a negative way, I don't mean it like that, but you remind me of my grandmother."

"Interesting," I said.

"I'm going to go ahead and ask you something. Have you become one of those macrobiotic people? Or vegans? I strongly recommend against it."

I couldn't tell if this was an acknowledgment of my alteration or just something else he was saying. No one else I saw that day had yet noticed anything. Though I had a five months pregnant classmate who had recently made a similar report: that no one had noticed.

And that was the day. I suppose I might have been more detained or disturbed by the change in my romantic prospects—either I had suffered a bad blow or, it was slimly possible, I'd received a tremendous boon—but I kind of knew where I was in my relationship cycle.

•

On Tuesdays, Wednesdays, and Fridays, when I had no afternoon classes, I worked at an after-school program for teenage girls, called GRLZ. Fridays were for Bardo exercises, which are "perceptual distortion" exercises. The week before, our Bardo exercise involved going to the grocery store with the goal of walking each aisle without touching anything, without buying anything, without even setting off the sensors for the automatic doors at the entrance, but, instead, following in and out other people who had set off the sensors. We spent an hour and a half like that. It was like practicing being a ghost.

The mechanism of Bardo activities is that they require total focus, but they also blank you out. I know these exercises sound stupid, I say to the girls, but they seem to work. Or at least to do something. The van ride home after the grocery store, for example, was very peaceful. Although one girl started crying. But in a very unobtrusive way. The girls in the program are—I wouldn't say they are "difficult." It is more that they have difficulties. Most of them are referred to GRLZ from the nearby pediatric clinic and have lupus, or eating disorders, or severe asthma, or early run-ins with alcohol and drugs.

That day we were staying close to home for Bardo. The local Mormon church provides GRLZ with a free space: a large, open-layout basement with pantry shelves holding gallon jars of peanut butter, vats of pickles, costumes from past Christmas pageants, cartons of colored pipe cleaners, hanks of yarn, reams of colored stationery, boxes whose labels cannot be trusted but that purport to contain Life cereal. I opened the Bardo notebook to a random page and began to read aloud from Activity #14: " 'Walk quietly around the space, touching nothing except the floor with your feet—' "

"We're all touching air all the time," interrupted Alina, the most frizzy-haired and isolated of the girls. "Air is a thing."

"That's true," I said. "Very good. OK, 'As you quietly walk around the space, pause to take note, almost like you're a camera taking pictures, of perspectives or places or things that remind you of being dead.' "

I did feel a slight jet stream of having stumbled into an "advanced" exercise. "Take special note of the particular words, OK?" I went on, following the script. "It's not about what reminds you *of death*. Or *of dying*. It says specifically: things that remind you of *being dead*. We can think about what that might mean."

That's when Brandee, who has lupus and nice manners, said to me, "You look sideways pregnant."

"I'm not pregnant, but thank you for asking."

"I didn't say pregnant, I said sideways pregnant."

"Do you guys have any questions about the exercise?" I asked. "Listen to your instincts. I'll set the egg timer for forty-five minutes. Then we'll regroup and discuss. Just try to relax into it." The setting was ideal for the exercise, really. The fluorescent lighting glanced off the steel refrigerator in a way that was like not being in Kansas anymore.

"That's what happens when you're a bulimia," another of the girls said. "The sideways thing."

"No," a third said. "When you're a bulimia, your teeth are black and you cough blood. That's where the idea of werewolves comes from, these hungry creatures with bloody mouths—"

"That's not true. In bulimia you explode out your ribs—"

"That bleeding mouth stuff is about being inbred, it's not bulimia—"

"I didn't mean to start a thing," quiet Brandee said.

I acknowledged to the girls that their curiosity and speculation were normal, even admirable. I made a simple announcement that it was a breast, what they were talking about. My hope was that we could then quickly move on.

"I think it looks hot," said Lucille, the one GRL who herself was especially "hot" and who, when she arrived two weeks earlier, had unsettled the group dynamics just by looking the way she did. She was of the physical type, already full and curvy, of whom I'd heard men say that she was so ripe that one had to take her now, before she was rotten. Lucille snapped a photo of me with her phone. I asked her nicely to please not do that. She took several more photos. At least I liked the navy color of the fitted long tee I was wearing. My face looks best against dark colors. I would need more of these longer shirts, I noted to myself. Lucille went on: "You know those models, they're all so, so flat, they have no breasts at all. They choose them as models because they look like young boys, you so totally know that's what all those gays running the industry are dreaming of, of a world where even women are boys, they're trying to convince *us* to wish we were boys, they're trying to make *us* think like *them*, and that is so, so wrong. It's like so wrong, and that's why it's so cool; it's like you're like saying, No, I am so definitely not a boy, not a man, very much not, like there's no denying it."

I repeated, to Lucille and to everyone, that I was setting the timer. I also reread the exercise prompt aloud, start to finish, one more time. I reemphasized that we were entering quiet Bardo time. And that was that. I sat on a costume trunk and waited for the minutes to pass. I like being near kids. It takes me out of myself; or, it does something. There had been a woman, Helen Magramm, whose children, two boys, I babysat when I was a teenager. I had no authority with those kids, and nearly every time one or both of them ended up crying before their parents returned home. I'm surprised neither was ever seriously hurt. One night years later, the boys were in high school, the husband woke up to his wife having a seizure in her sleep. It turned out she had a brain tumor. The tumor was resected and she recovered. Three years later the younger son was killed in a car accident. Eventually the mom, in her forties, was put in a nursing home, after a return of the tumor. I'd probably lived in seven different towns after I had last seen Helen Magramm; that was why, I think, I very rarely thought of her; I was away from almost all the triggers that might bring me back to being a teenager. Not too long ago, Helen appeared briefly in one of my dreams; and a couple of days later my mother told me Helen had died. That spooked me, naturally.

.

I decided to go see a professional about the breast.

The doctor had thick, long blond hair and a mild Russian accent; when she palpated my neck, a scent of eucalyptus that must have been her hand lotion or soap came to me. I trusted this doctor because a few months earlier I'd come to her about an intermittent ear pain I'd had for years—it was always in the same ear, and the pain was worse in the mornings, but I couldn't predict which mornings it would be there—and with no fuss or imaging she had determined that my ear pain was heartburn manifesting as ear pain. A diagnostic trial of Prilosec had disappeared the problem. She told me an apparently-so story about how long ago, in an early pre-embryonic state, the ear's nerve and the esophagus's nerve had been intimates, and that it was a memory of this closeness that made the two areas confuse their pains, and that this intimacy persisted even as they were now distant. It was a fanciful, pastel-hued story, yes, but I mean, she cured me. After that solve, Dr. Jane Shliakhtsitsava seemed to me like a dragon slayer.

Also, I couldn't help trusting her because she was very pretty.

I mentally absented myself as she examined the dorsal breast.

She asked me about heart palpitations, about night sweats, rapid weight gains, rapid weight losses. "Any major regrets?" she asked.

"I don't think so," I said.

"Losses you haven't accepted?"

"Not really. I mean, I'm far from home. But I guess we're all far, right?"

"Have you been trying to have children or adopt children? Or thinking about it?"

"No."

"Have you lost a child?"

"Never."

"Have you lost a loved one? Or love? Are you longing for your childhood?"

"I don't get your line of questions," I said.

"I ask these things," she began, and her accent suddenly sounded false to me, "because it's very common to manifest these things in our body. It's nothing to be ashamed about. Your body speaks a language. It's like a foreign language we all speak but have forgotten how to understand. Maybe you've heard of pseudocyesis, of women who develop all the signs and symptoms of pregnancy, even though they aren't pregnant. There's no shame in speaking in signs. You shouldn't worry about the word 'hysteria.' It's not just women who speak these languages. I think men are even more fluent in them—"

"Did you do your training in Oregon?"

"In Vladivostok," she said. "But I'm always training. Even now I'm training."

"I just want you to say whether I'm dying or not dying. Really, that's it."

She took out a green marker pen from her lab coat and wrote down two words in all caps on the white butcher paper of the exam table. "I understand you're more interested in *prognosis* than *diagnosis*," she said, indicating the two words she had written. She paused. "That's natural. I understand that. But I'm not so detained by either diagnosis or prognosis; what really interests me is simply *gnosis*." She had underlined and was pointing to the stacked "gnosis" ends of the two words. "Gnosis itself."

There had once been a TV show in which a gnu named Gary Gnu reported the gnews. "It seems like you don't believe in illness," I said.

"I believe in wellness," Dr. Shliakhtsitsava said.

Her framed diplomas suggested she was normally certified; also, she had helped me before; you can't be blinded to past goodness by the klieg lights of a little bit of odd.

"But do you think I can get it safely removed?" I asked. "Do you think my insurance will cover the surgery? It's not considered just cosmetic, is it? I mean, it's a pretty extreme case if it is. Would I need full anesthesia?"

"I can answer all those questions for you," she said, deploying full eye contact. "And I will answer all those questions for you. But first I want to say"—and here her status as a pretty person seemed to flush her face with ordained assuredness—"you might want to think about this new part of yourself. Just take some time and think about it. Do you really want to change yourself just to suit fashion when you don't even know what fashion will bring next? That may not be the person you want to be."

The visit cost me $215. I appreciated that she had taken the time to really talk to me.

.

Spring came around. Flowers, I suspect they were daffodils, made their pronouncements. What were maybe dogwood blossoms decorated neighborhood trees. I started craving fruit popsicles. One evening, on the street, I by chance met a woman I had known back when I was in high school. She had distinctively large and wide-set eyes and had never seemed to have reached puberty; it might have been a medical thing; anyhow, it made her easy to recognize. She was in town to help design a duck pond for the campus, or really it was a sort of goose pond, she explained, a place to encourage Canadian geese to rest during their annual migrations. What a treat to see you, she said. You know, I wanted to write to you, she went on. To make sure you were OK. But I didn't want you to feel singled out in that way. I hadn't talked to you for so many years.

Don't worry about it, I said. I'm just happy to have run into you.

I had no idea what she might be talking about. That evening I went ahead and investigated myself on the Internet.

Someone, probably one of the GRLZ, or one of the GRLZ's friends, had pinned one of the more casually striking photos of my "condition" onto her Pinterest, which had gone to a number of other Pinterests, and Tumblrs, and other places I didn't know about, and those images had synapsed and traveled and collided with other images, and commentary, and eventually become a Buzzfeed, yoked alongside what must have really driven the traffic, a photo of an actress from a remake of the movie *Total Recall*; the woman—she played an alien or something—was three breasts across and wore an outfit that offered coverage of those breasts only via a strap across the nipples. She was fairly inarguably hot. Although somewhat arguably, as manifested in the comments sections. However, the majority of the censoriousness, ridicule, and loving support was directed not at the altered beauty from a fictional dystopic 2084 in a red dress and thigh-high black leather boots but, rather, at me. I was an ugly who needed to get over herself, or someone bravely making my own choices, or a fourth-wave feminist, or a symptom of fakesterdom, or a rebel against the tyranny of the "natural," or a person who really, really needed help . . . It was unclear what I would learn if I read more, and I wasn't sure I wanted to learn it. Though I did like one comment, in which someone wondered whether this was "a difference that made a difference." He/she posited that that was what knowledge was: a difference that made a difference. The next comment compared me with eugenicists. I stopped reading. I wrote to administrators of the first few sites I had come across, in the cases where I was able to find a contact address; I asked, politely, if my photo could be taken down. It was, after all, a photo of me, an ordinary citizen who had not put herself forward. Only one person wrote back to me. He expressed understanding. He said he admired my courage in making a physical "statement," and he invited me to participate in an interview series he curated, American Innovations, on his YouTube channel. There were *freedoms from* and *freedoms to*, he said. That was what made this country great, he said. Past participants had included the celebrity underwear designer Lorna Drew and the winner of *Survivor Panama* Aras Baskaukas.

I had once seen a hog at a farm. That hog must have weighed near on two thousand pounds, and she was in a little pen—not the worst conditions, merely depressing ones—and there were sores near her tail, which seemed to have been clipped off; the sores had attracted flies; she had many nipples, and they also looked like sores, and might have been cohabiting space with sores; her babies were not with her; she was quiet in her pen. I describe this because that was how I felt. I came across stories connecting soy consumption to extra-mammary development; another story of a plastic surgeon in Los Angeles who combined belly button removal with breast addition in a package deal. In Germany, some male soldiers were developing enlarged breasts from the repetitive recoil of shooting rifles. I'm not one of these people who are disheartened that the universe is expanding. But as news and data breed and the crowded channels grow ever noisier, I do feel that the space is ever increasing between me and it, whatever it might be. I didn't call up my mom, or my aunt, or my previous boyfriend, or any of the boyfriends before that, either. I didn't make a Facebook posting on which others might comment with generous sympathy. But I did feel very feminine. I went out and bought a mod kind of dress, sort of like a shift.

WILD BERRY BLUE

This is a story about my love for Roy, though first I have to say a few words about my dad, who was there with me at the Mc-Donald's every Saturday, letting his little girl, I was maybe nine, swig his extra half-and-halfs, stack the shells into messy towers. My dad drank from his bottomless cup of coffee and read the paper while I dipped my McDonaldland cookies in milk and pretended to read the paper. He wore gauzy striped button-ups with pearline snaps. He had girlish wrists, a broad forehead like a Roman, a terrifying sneeze.

"How's the coffee?" I'd ask.

"Not good, not bad. How's the milk?"

"Terrific," I'd say. Or maybe "Exquisite."

My mom was at home cleaning the house; our job there at the McDonald's was to be out of her way.

And that's how it always was on Saturdays. We were Jews, we had our rituals. That's how I think about it. Despite being secular Israelis living in the wilds of Oklahoma, an ineluctable part in us still indulged certain repetitions.

·

Many of the people who worked at the McDonald's were former patients of my dad's: mostly drug addicts and alcoholics in rehab programs. A few plain old depressions. An occasional paranoid. The McDonald's hired people no one else would hire; I think it was a policy. My dad, in effect, was the

McDonald's–Psychiatric Institute liaison. The McDonald's manager, a deeply Christian man, would regularly come over and say hello to us and thank my dad for many things. Once he thanked him for, as a Jew, having kept safe the word of God during all the dark years.

"I'm not sure I've done so much," my dad had answered.

"But it's been living there in you," the manager said. He was a nice man, admirably tolerant of the accompanying dramas of his workforce, dramas I picked up on peripherally. Absenteeism, petty theft, once a worker ODing in the bathroom. I had no idea what that meant, to OD, but it sounded spooky. "They slip out from under their own control," I heard the manager say, and the phrase stuck with me. I pictured the right side of a person lifting up a velvet rope and leaving the left side behind.

.

Sometimes, dipping my McDonaldland cookies—FryGuy, Grimace—I'd hold a cookie in the milk too long and it would saturate and crumble to the bottom of the carton. There it was something mealy, vulgar. Horrible. I'd lose my appetite. Though the surface of the milk often remained pristine, I could feel the cookie's presence down below, lurking. Like some ancient bottom-dwelling fish with both eyes on one side of its head.

I'd tip the carton back slowly in order to see what I dreaded seeing, just to feel that queasiness, and also the pre-queasiness of knowing the main queasiness was coming, the anticipatory ill. Beautiful, Horrible: I had a running mental list. Cleaning lint from the screen of the dryer—beautiful. Bright glare on glass—horrible. Mealworms—also horrible. The stubbles of shaved hair in a woman's armpit—beautiful.

The Saturday I was to meet Roy, after dropping a cookie

in the milk, I looked over, up at my dad. "Cookie," I squeaked,
turning a sour face at the carton.

He pulled out his worn leather wallet, with its inexplica-
ble rust stain ring on the front. He gave me a dollar. My mom
never gave me money, and my dad always gave me more than
I needed. (He also called me the Queen of Sheba sometimes,
like when I'd stand up on a dining room chair to see how things
looked from there.) The torn corner of the bill he gave me
was held on with yellowed Scotch tape. Someone had written
on the dollar in blue pen, over the Treasury seal, "I love
Becky!!!"

I go up to the counter with the Becky dollar to buy my
replacement milk, and what I see is a tattoo, most of which I
can't see. A starched white long-sleeve shirt covers most of it.
But a little blue-black lattice of it I can see—a fragment like
ancient elaborate metalwork, that creeps down all the way,
past the wrist, to the back of the hand, kinking up and over a
very plump vein. The vein is so distended I imagine laying my
cheek on it in order to feel the blood pulse and flow, to maybe
even hear it. Beautiful. So beautiful. I don't know why but I'm
certain this tattoo reaches all the way up to his shoulder. His
skin is deeply tanned but the webbing between his fingers sooty
pale.

This beautiful feeling. I haven't had it about a person before. Not in this way.

In a trembling moment I shift my gaze up to the engraved
nametag. There's a yellow *M* emblem, then "Roy."

·

I place my dollar down on the counter. I put it down like it's a
password I'm unsure of, one told to me by an unreliable source.
"Milk," I say, quietly.

Roy, whose face I finally look at, is staring off, up, over

past my head, like a bored lifeguard. He hasn't heard or noticed me, little me, the only person on line. Roy is biting his lower lip and one of his teeth, one of the canines, is much whiter than the others. Along his cheekbones his skin looks dry and chalky. His eyes are blue, with bruisy, beautiful eyelids.

I try again, a little bit louder. "Milk."

Still he doesn't hear me; I begin to feel as if maybe I am going to cry because of these accumulated moments of being nothing. That's what it feels like standing so close to this type of beauty—like being nothing.

Resolving to give up if I'm not noticed soon I make one last effort and, leaning over on my tiptoes, I push the dollar farther along the counter, far enough that it tickles Roy's thigh, which is leaned up against the counter's edge.

He looks down at me, startled, then laughs abruptly. "Hi little sexy," he says. Then he laughs again, too loud, and the other cashier, who has one arm shrunken and paralyzed, turns and looks and then looks away again.

These few seconds seem like everything that has ever happened to me.

My milk somehow purchased, I go back to the table wondering if I am green, or emitting a high-pitched whistling sound, or dead.

.

It's not actually the first time I've seen Roy I realize back at the table as, with great concentration, I dip my Hamburglar cookie into the cool milk. I think that maybe I've seen Roy— that coarse blond hair—every Saturday, for all my Saturdays. I take a bite from my cookie. I have definitely seen him before. Just somehow not in this way.

My dad appears to be safely immersed in whatever is on the other side of the crossword puzzle and bridge commentary page. I feel—a whole birch tree pressing against my inner

walls, its leaves reaching to the top of my throat—the awful
sense of wanting some other life. I have thought certain boys
in my classes have pretty faces, but I have never before felt like
laying my head down on the vein of a man's wrist. (I still think
about that vein sometimes.) Almost frantically I wonder if Roy
can see me there at my table, there with my dad, where I've
been seemingly all my Saturdays.

Attempting to rein in my anxiety I try to think: What
makes me feel this way? Possessed like this? Is it a smell in the
air? It just smells like beefy grease. Which is pleasant enough
but nothing new. A little mustard. A small vapor of disinfec-
tant. I wonder obscurely if actually Roy is Jewish, as if that
might make normal this spiraling fated feeling. As if really
what's struck me is just an unobvious family resemblance. But
I know that we're almost the only Jews in town.

Esther married the gentile king, I think in a desperate absurd flash.

Since a part of me wants to stay forever I finish my cookies quickly.

"Let's go," I say.

"Already?"

"Can't we just leave? Let's leave."

·

There's the Medieval Fair, I think to myself in consolation
all Sunday. It's two weekends away. You're always happy at
the Medieval Fair, I say to myself, as I fail to enjoy sorting
my stamps, fail to stand expectantly, joyfully, on the dining
room chair. Instead I fantasize about running the french fry
fryer in the back of McDonald's. I imagine myself learning
to construct Happy Meal boxes in a breath, to fold the papers
around the hamburgers just so. I envision a stool set out for
me to climb atop so that I can reach the apple fritter dis-
penser; Roy spots me, making sure I don't fall. And I get a

tattoo. Of a bird, or a fish, or a ring of birds and fish, around my ankle.

There is no happiness in these daydreams. Just an over-crowded and feverish empty.

At school on Monday I sit dejectedly in the third row of Mrs. Brown's class because that is where we are on the weekly seating chart rotation. I suffer through exercises in long division, through bits about Magellan. Since I'm not in the front, I'm able to mark most of my time drawing a tremen-dous maze, one that stretches to the outer edges of the note-book paper. This while the teacher reads to us from something about a girl and her horse. Something. A horse. Who cares! Who cares about a horse! I think, filled, suddenly, with unex-pected rage. That extra-white tooth. The creeping chain of the tattoo. I try so hard to be dedicated to my maze, pressing my pencil sharply into the paper as if to hold down my focus better.

All superfluous, even my sprawling maze, superfluous. A flurry of pencil shavings—they come out as if in a breath—from the sharpener distracts me. A sudden phantom pain near my elbow consumes my attention.

I crumple up my maze dramatically, do a basketball throw to the wastebasket like the boys do. I miss, of course, but no one seems to notice, which is the nature of my life at school, where I am only noticed in bland, embarrassing ways, like when a substitute teacher can't pronounce my name. The joy-lessness of my basketball toss, it makes me look over at my once-crush Josh Deere and feel sad for him, for the smallness of his life.

One day, I think, it will be Saturday again.

But time seemed to move so slowly. I'd lost my appetite for certain details of life.

·

"Do you know about that guy at McDonald's with the one really white tooth?" I brave this question to my dad. This during a commercial break from *Kojak*.

"Roy's a recovering heroin addict," my dad says, turning to stare at me. He's always said things to me other people wouldn't have said to kids. He'd already told me about the Oedipus complex, and I had stared dully back at him. He would defend General Rommel to me, though I had no idea who General Rommel was. He'd make complex points about the strait of Bosporus.

So he said that to me, about Roy, which obviously he shouldn't have said. (Here, years later, I still think about the mystery of that plump vein, which seems a contradiction. Which occasionally makes me wonder if there were two Roys.)

"I don't know what the story with the tooth is," my dad adds. "Maybe it's false?" And then it's back to the mystery of *Kojak*.

I wander into the kitchen feeling unfulfilled and so start interrogating my mom about my Purim costume, for the carnival that is still two Sundays, aeons, away. The Purim carnival is in Tulsa, over an hour's driving distance; I don't know the kids there, and my costume never measures up. "And the crown," I remind her hollowly. I'm not quite bold enough to bring up that she could buy me one of the beautiful ribbon crowns sold at the Medieval Fair, which we'll be at the day before. "I don't want," I mumble mostly to myself, "one of those paper crowns that everyone has."

•

Thursday night I am at the Skaggs Alpha Beta grocery with my mom. I am lingering amid all the sugar cereals I know will never come home with me. It's only every minute or so that I am thinking about Roy's hand, about how he called me sexy.

Then I see Roy. He has no cart, no basket. He's holding a

gallon of milk and a supersize Twizzlers and he is reaching for, I can't quite see—a big oversize box that looks to be Honeycomb. A beautiful assemblage. Beautiful.

I turn away from Roy. I feel my whole body, even my ears, blushing. The backs of my hands feel itchy the way they always do in spring. I touch the cool metal shelving, run my fingers up and over the plastic slipcovers, over the price labels, hearing every nothing behind me. The price labels make a sandy sliding sound when I push them. He's a monster, Roy. Not looking at him, just feeling that power he has over me, a monster.

My mom in lace-up sandals cruises by the aisle with our shopping cart. The lighting seems to change. Able now to turn around, I see that Roy is gone. I run after my mom. When finally we're in the car again, back door closed on the groceries—when I turn around, I see celery stalks innocently sticking out of a brown paper bag—I feel great relief.

.

I decide to wash my feet in the sink; this always makes me happy. On my dad's shaving mirror in the bathroom, old Scotch tape holding it in place, is a yellowed bit of paper, torn from a magazine. For years it's been there, inscrutable. Now I feel certain it carries a secret. About love maybe. About the possessed feeling I have because of Roy.

It says *And human speech is but a cracked kettle upon which we tap crude rhythms for bears to dance to, while we long to make music that—*

Next to the scrap is a sticker of mine, of a green apple.

I look again at the quote: the bears, the kettle.

Silly, I decide. It's all very silly. I start to dry my feet with a towel.

For the impending McDonald's Saturday I resolve to walk

right past my tattooed crush. I'll have nothing to do with him, with his hi little sexys. This denouncement is actually extraordinarily painful since Roy alone is now my whole world. Everything that came before— my coin collection in the Tupperware, the corrugated cardboard trim on school bulletin boards, the terror of the fire pole—now revealed supremely childish and vain. Without even deciding to, I have left all that and now must leave Roy, too. I commit to enduring the burden of the universe alone. The universe with its mysterious General Rommels, its heady strait of Bosporus. I resolve to suffer.

.

Saturday comes again. My mom has already taken the burner covers off the stove and set them in the sink. I'm trying the think-about-the-Medieval-Fair trick so as to not think about maybe seeing Roy. I picture the ducks at the duck pond, the way they waddle right up and snatch the bread slice right out of my hand. I focus on the fair, knowing that time will move forward in that way, eventually waddle forward to the next weekend.

Buckling myself into the front seat of our yellow Pinto, I put an imitation Life Savers under my tongue, a blue one. When my dad walks in front of the car on the way to the driver's side, I notice that he has slouchy shoulders. Horrible. Not his shoulders. But my noticing them.

"I love you," I say to my dad. He laughs and says that's good. I sit there hating myself a little.

I concentrate on my candy, on letting it be there, letting it do its exquisitely slow melt under my tongue. Beautiful. I keep that same candy the whole car ride over, through stop signs, waiting for a kid on a bigwheel to cross, past the Conoco, with patience during the long wait for the final left turn. In my pocket I have more candies. Most of a roll of wild berry.

When I move my tongue just a tiny bit, the flavor, the sugary slur, assaults my sensations. I choke on a little bit of saliva.

.

When we enter I sense Roy at our left; I walk on the far side of my dad, hoping to hide in his shadow. In a hush I inform him that I'll go save our table and that he should order me the milk and the cookies.

"OK," he whispers back, as if this were just some game.

At the table I stare straight ahead at the molded plastic bench, summoning all my meagernesses together so as to keep from looking feverishly around. I think I sense Roy's blond hair off in the distance to my left. In weakness I glimpse sideways; I see a potted plant.

"How's the coffee?" I ask after my dad has settled in across from me.

He shrugs his ritual shrug, but no words except the question of how is your milk. Is he mad at me? As I begin dipping my cookies in anguish I answer that the milk is delicious.

Why do we say these little things? I wonder. Why do I always want the McDonaldland butter cookies and never the chocolate chip? It seems creepy to me now for the first time, all the habits and ways of the heart I have that I didn't choose for myself.

I throw back three half-and-halfs.

"Will you get me some more half-and-halfs?" my dad asks.

He asks nicely. And he is really reading the paper while I am not. Of course I'm going to go get creamers. I'm a kid, I remember.

"I don't feel well," I try.

"Really?"

"I mean I feel fine," I say, getting out of the chair.

•

Roy. Taking a wild berry candy from my pocket, I resolve again to focus on a candy under my tongue instead of on him. I head first toward the back wall, darting betwixt and between the tables with their attached swiveling chairs. This is the shiniest, cleanest place in town; that's what McDonald's was like back then. Even the corners and crevices are clean. Our house: even after my mom cleans, it's all still in disarray. I'll unfold a blanket and find a stray sock inside. Behind the toilet there's blue lint. Maybe that's what makes a home, I think, its special type of mess.

And then I'm at the front counter. I don't look up.

I stand off to the side since I'm not really ordering anything, just asking for a favor, not paying for milk but asking for creamers. Waiting to be noticed, I stare down at the brushed steel counter with its flattering hazy reflection, and then it appears, he appears. I see first his palm, reflected in the steel. Then I see his knuckles, the hairs on the back of his hand, the lattice tattoo, the starched shirt cuff that is the beginning of hiding all the rest of the tattoo that I can't see.

Beautiful.

A part of me decides I am taking him back into my heart. Even if no room will be left for anything else.

Roy notices me. He leans down, eyes level with my sweaty curls stuck against my forehead, at the place where I know I have my birthmark, a dark brown mole there above my left eyebrow, and he says, his teeth showing, his strange glowing white canine showing: "Need something, sweets?' He taps my nose with his finger.

That candy, I had forgotten about it, and I move my tongue and the flavor—it all comes rushing out, overwhelming, and I drool a little bit as I blurt out, "I'm going to the Medieval Fair next weekend." I wipe my wet lips with the back of my hand and see the wild berry blue saliva staining.

"Cool," he says, straightening up. He interlaces his fingers and pushes them outward, and they crack deliciously, and I think about macadamias. I think I see him noticing the blue smeared on my right hand. He says then: "I love those puppets they sell there—those real plain wood ones."

I just stare at Roy's blue eyes. I love blue eyes. Still to this day I am always telling myself that I don't like them, that I find them lifeless and dull and that I prefer brown eyes, like mine, like my parents', but it's a lie. It's a whole other wilder type of love that I feel for these blue-eyed people of the world. So I look up at him, at those blue eyes, and I'm thinking about those plain wooden puppets—this is all half a second—then the doors open behind me and that invasive heat enters and the world sinks down, mud and mush and the paste left behind by cookies.

"Oh," I say. "Half-and-half."

He reaches into a tray of much melted ice and bobbing creamers and he hands three to me. My palm burns where he touched me and my vision is blurry; only the grooves on the half-and-half container keep me from vanishing.

"Are you going to the fair?" I brave. Heat in my face again, the feeling just before a terrible rash. I'm already leaving the counter so as not to see those awful blue eyes, and I hear, "Ah, I'm working," and I don't even turn around.

I read the back of my dad's newspaper. They have found more fossils at the Spiro Mounds. There's no explanation for how I feel.

•

How can I describe the days of the next week? I'd hope to see Roy when I ran out to check the mail. I'd go drink from the hose in our front yard thinking he might walk or drive by, even though I had no reason to believe he might ever come to our neighborhood. I got detention for not turning in my book report of "The Yellow Wallpaper." I found myself rummaging around in my father's briefcase, as if Roy's files—I imagined the yellow "Confidential" envelope from Clue—might somehow be there. Maybe I don't need to explain because who hasn't been overtaken by this shade of love? I remember walking home from school very slowly, anxiously, as if through foreign, unpredictable terrain. I wanted to buy Roy a puppet at the Medieval Fair. One of the wooden ones like he'd mentioned. Only in that thought could I rest. All the clutter of my mind was waiting to come closer to that moment of purchasing a puppet.

So I did manage to wake up in the mornings. I did try to go to sleep at night. Though my heart seemed to be racing to its own obscure rhythm, private even from me.

Friday night before the fair, my bedroom alien and lurksome, I was hopeless for rest. After pulling my maze workbook down from the shelf, I went into the brightly lit bathroom. I turned on the overhead fan so that it would become noisy enough to overwhelm the sound in my mind of Roy cracking his knuckles. The whirring fan noise: it was like a quiet. Sitting in the empty tub, I set the maze book on the rounded ledge and purposely began on a difficult page. I worked cautiously, tracing ahead with my finger before setting pen to paper. This was pleasing, though out of the corner of my eye I saw the yellowed magazine fragment—*cracked kettle*—and it was like a ghost in the room with me, though its message, I felt sure—almost too sure, considering that I didn't understand it—had nothing to do with me.

In the morning my mom found me there in the tub, like some passed-out drunk, my maze book open on my small chest. I must have fallen asleep. I felt like crying, didn't even know why. I reached up to my face, wondering if something had gone wrong with it.

"Do you have a fever?" my mom asked.

When she left, assured, somewhat, I tried out those words— *Human speech is like a cracked kettle*—as if they were the coded answer to a riddle.

I was always that kind of kid who crawled into bed with her parents, who felt safe only with them. If my mom came into my classroom because I had forgotten my lunch at home, I wasn't ashamed, like other kids were, but proud. For a few years of my life, up until then, my desires hadn't chased away from me. I wanted to fall asleep on the sofa while my dad watched *The Rockford Files*, and so I did. I wanted couscous with butter, and so I had some. Yes sometimes shopping with my mom I coveted a pair of overalls, or a frosted cookie, but the want would be faint, and fade as soon as we'd walked away.

·

We had left the house uncleaned when we went to the fair that Saturday. I was thinking about the wooden puppet, but I felt obligated to hope for a crown; that's what I was supposed to be pining for. I imagined that my mom would think to buy me a crown for my Queen Esther costume. But maybe, I hoped, she would forget all about the crown. It wasn't unlikely. What seemed like the world to me often revealed itself, through her eyes, to be nothing.

I had always loved the Medieval Fair. A woman dressed up in an elaborate mermaid costume would sit under the bridge that spanned the artificial pond. People tossed quarters down at her. I thought she was beautiful. She'd flap her tail, wave coyly. It wasn't until years later that I realized that she was considered trashy. Farther on there was a stacked hay maze that had already become too easy by late elementary school, but I liked looking at it from a distance, from up on the small knoll. I think every turn you might take was fine. Whichever way you went you still made it out. It was upsetting, being spat out so soon.

We saw the dress-up beggar with the prosthetic nose and warts. We crossed the bridge, saw the mermaid. A pale teenage boy in stonewashed jeans and a tank top leaned against the bridge's railing, smoking and looking down at her. Two corseted women farther along sang bawdy ballads in the shade of a willow and while we listened a slouchy man went by with a gigantic foam mallet. The whole world, it seemed, was laughing or fighting or crying or unfolding chairs or blending smoothies and this would go on eternally. Vendors sold wooden flutes, Jacob's ladders, feathered mobiles. In an open field two ponies and three sheep were there for the petting and the overseer held a baby pig in his hands. We ate fresh ears of boiled corn, smothered with butter and cracked pepper. My mom didn't mention the price. That really did make it feel like a day in some other me's life.

But I felt so unsettled. Roy's tooth in my mind as I bit into the corn, Roy's fingers on my palm as I thrummed my hand along a low wooden fence. I had so little of Roy and yet he had all of me and the feeling ran deep to the most ancient parts of me. So much so that I felt that my love for Roy shamed my people, whoever my people were, whoever I was queen of, people I had never met, nervous people and sad people and dead people, all clambering for air and space inside me. I didn't even know what I wanted from Roy. I still don't. All my life love has felt like a croquet mallet to the head. Something absurd, ready for violence. Love.

I remember once years later, in a love fit, stealing cherry Luden's cough drops from a convenience store. I had the money to pay for them but I instead stole them. I wanted a cheap childish cherry flavor on my tongue when I saw my love, who of course isn't my love anymore. That unrelenting pathetic euphoria. Low-quality cough drops. That's how I felt looking around anxiously for the wooden puppet stand, how I felt looking twice at every blond man who passed, wondering if he might somehow be Roy, there for me, even though he'd said he wouldn't be there. Thinking about that puppet for Roy eclipsed all other thoughts. Put a slithery veil over the whole day. How much would the puppet cost? I didn't have my own pocket money, an allowance or savings or anything like that. I wasn't in the habit of asking for things. I never asked for toys. I never asked for sugar cereals. I felt to do so was wrong. I had almost cried that one day just whispering to myself about the crown. But all I wanted was that puppet because that puppet was going to solve everything.

.

At the puppet stand I lingered. I was hoping that one of my parents would take notice of the puppets, pick one up. My dad, standing a few paces away, stood out from the crowd in his button-up shirt. He looked weak, sunbeaten. My mom was at my side, her arms folded across a tank top that was emergency orange. It struck me, maybe for the first time, that they came to this fair just for me.

"I've never wanted anything this much in my whole life," I confessed in a rush, my hand on the unfinished wood of one of the puppets. "I want this more than a crown."

My mom laughed at me, or at the puppet. "It's so ugly," she said, in Hebrew.

"That's not true," I whispered furiously, feeling as if every-thing had fallen silent, as if the ground beneath me were shift-ing. The vendor must surely have understood my mom, by her tone alone. I looked over at him: a fat bearded man talking to a long-haired barefoot princess. He held an end of her dusty hair distractedly; his other hand he had inside the collar of his shirt. He was sweating.

"It's junk," my mom said.

"You don't like anything," I said, nearly screaming, there in the bright sun. "You never like anything at all." My mother turned her back to me. I sensed the vendor turn our way.

"I'll get it for you," my dad said, suddenly right with us. There followed an awkward argument between my parents, which seemed only to heighten my dad's pleasure in taking out his rust-stained wallet, in standing his ground, in being irrevocably on my side.

His alliance struck me as misguided, pathetic, even childish; I felt like a villain; we bought the puppet.

That dumb puppet—I carried it around in its wrinkly green plastic bag. For some reason I found myself haunted by the word "leprosy." When we watched the minstrel show in the little outdoor amphitheater, I tried to forget the green bag under the bench. We only made it a few steps before my mom noticed it was gone. She went back and fetched it.

At home I noticed that the wood of one of the hands of the puppet was cracked. That wasn't the only reason I couldn't give the puppet to Roy. Looking at that mute piece of wood, I saw something. A part of me that I'd never chosen, that I would never control. I went to the bathroom, turned on the loud fan, and cried. An image of Roy came to my mind, particularly of that tooth. I felt my love falling off, dissolving.

He was my first love, my first love in the way that first loves are usually second or third or fourth loves. I still think about a stranger in a green jacket across from me in the waiting room at the DMV. About a blue-eyed man with a singed earlobe that I saw at a Baskin-Robbins with his daughter. My first that kind of love. I never got over him. I never get over anyone.

THE ENTIRE NORTHERN SIDE
WAS COVERED WITH FIRE

They say no one reads anymore, but I find that's not the case. Prisoners read. I guess they're not given much access to computers. A felicitous injustice for me. The nicest reader letters I've received—also the only reader letters I've received—have come from prisoners. Maybe we're all prisoners? In our lives, our habits, our relationships? That's not nice, my saying that. Maybe it's even evil, to co-opt the misery of others.

I want to mention that, when I sold the movie, my husband had just left me. I came home one day and a bunch of stuff was gone. I thought we'd been robbed. Then I found a note: "I can't live here anymore." He had taken quite a lot with him. For example, we had a particularly nice Parmesan grater and he had taken that. But he had left behind his winter coat. Also a child. We had a child together, sort of. I was carrying it—girl or boy, I hadn't wanted to find out—inside me.

I searched online for a replacement for that Parmesan grater because I had really liked that Parmesan grater. It was that kind that works like a mill, not the kind you just scrape against; it had a handle that was fun to turn. There were a number of similar graters available but with unappealing "comfort" grips. Finally, I found the same model. Was it premature to repurchase? Two days passed basically like that. Then, on Wednesday, my brother called. I gave him the update on my life.

"Wow, that's really something," he said.

"Yeah. It is something."

Then he said, "I thought it was a work of fantasy, Trish. I mean, I guess I should have told you about it—"

"What?"

"The blog," he said. "His blog. I-Can't-Stand-My-Wife-Dot-Blogspot-Dot-Com—"

"Are you going through one of your sleepless phases again?"

"Trish, I know it makes me sound snoopy, but Jonathan always seemed a little off to me, you know? So after he left your apartment one time, when I was alone there, I don't know, I'm sorry, I opened up his laptop, and I looked through the browser history. I was curious about his porn. I thought maybe there would be some really weird porn—"

"There was weird porn?"

"None at all. Which in itself was kind of weird. No porn. Just his blog. And—"

"All right. Well. I'm thinking of buying a new Parmesan grater—"

"I thought it was satire, Trish. It's pretty funny. Look, I knew you could never have said some of that stuff. I mean, you are kind of critical, Trish, but still. How could I have known Jonathan was serious? I thought, Maybe these things can be healthy. Funny is healthy. Maybe this is a healthy way for Jonathan to vent some anger, some hurt feelings. Healthy fantasy, you know? I didn't know what to do, Trish. I asked my shrink. He wouldn't weigh in! I decided not to interfere. Look, don't be mad at me, Trish, I'm just the traumatized bystander here—"

"You keep saying Trish. You do that when you're trying to avoid something. You should just come out and say whatever it is you want to say instead of saying Trish all the time."

"I'm going to come over and we're going to read it together. Or not. If that's what you want. Whatever you want."

I wasn't going to read the blog. So much writing out there in the world and who wants to read it? Not me.

.

All of this was not long after the publication of my first novel, and I had some money, even a bit of dignity, as the novel had been somewhat successful; at least, I'd been given a decent advance and some money from foreign rights, too—it was a dream!—but I didn't have *lots* of dignity and I didn't have lots of money, either, just some. The novel was a love story, between a bird and a whale. Why was I already low on money? Partially because money just flies, as they say, or I guess it's time they say about that, the flying, but money, too. Very winged. Still, one of the main reasons I didn't have much money was that I had been paying my husband's way through business school. At least, I'd thought I was doing that, but it turned out he wasn't enrolled in school—I went to look for him, of course—and he had just been making those "tuition" withdrawals for himself. He did have many nice qualities, my husband. His hair unwashed was a heaven for me. He never asked me what I'd gotten done on any particular day. We'd fallen madly in love in three weeks; that had been fun. He used to call me little chicken. I still miss him.

But back to the point. I had some money but not lots of money. Prison bars of not-money grew around me in dreams, like wild magic corn. My agent called—so nice to be called by a friend! . . . or, no, not a friend . . . but sort of a friend!—to see if I was interested in taking a meeting with some "movie people." I started crying, and then we got past that. The meeting would just be to talk over a few notions, no biggie, but maybe. They had liked the screenplay adaptation of my novel—I hadn't written a screenplay adaptation, this seemed to be a confusion—but thought it would be too expensive to have underwater filming and also flight filming. They wanted a cheaper love story. What if it was two land animals? Anyway, a meeting was proposed. My agent acted as if I might find it beneath me, like only another novel was serious work, and even though I know he didn't really think that my writing was too serious to be set aside for a movie, I thought it was nice of him to pretend as if that might be the case.

"Great, great," I said, in a closing voice. "I'm, you know, all over that, totally."

"Totally?"

I coughed, as if to locate the problem in my throat.

"So you're OK?"

"Excited. I'll be there."

"Like even what's just happened to you—that's an idea right there."

•

And it struck me that maybe the meeting was the kind of thing that was going to save me, or at least that I should not entirely neglect to prepare for it, since it might kind of sort of save me a little bit. It could be a very good thing. I could watch myself put forward my best effort and then feel good about myself for having done so, for having tried. The least I could do, for me—and for my progeny, too!—was open up a Word file. Or, failing that, jot down a few notes on a legal pad. Let me just say now, because I don't believe in suspense—or at least I feel dirty when I try to engage in it, probably mostly because I'm no good at it—that I didn't prepare for the meeting at all.

My friend David came by. He needed to borrow money. He had much worse luck in life than I did. Also expensive dental problems, and an addiction to acupuncture. I told him about the leaving and also about the blog.

He already knew about the blog. He, too, had found it by going through the browser history of Jonathan's laptop. "The guy had a pretty fantastic imagination," David said. "I wouldn't have guessed it. I supposed we should respect that."

"Why didn't you tell me?"

"Remember the two months you didn't speak to me after I'd said maybe you were rash to marry after three weeks?"

I had recently heard someone use the word "poleaxed." That word made me think back to those years in Kentucky as a child; I don't know why, that was the thought. I was a fancy citified woman now, and so my life could have properly sized disasters, ones in the comedy-of-manners way of things, rather than in the losing-a-limb-to-a-tractor-blade way of things; that was another thought. If there was no blood on the floor, then it wasn't a tragedy. That was what "urban" meant. Could mean. Poleaxed. I had also once come across a phrase about a book "lying like a poleaxed wildebeest in the middle of my life." It was my life that was lying in the middle of my life like that, like a poleaxed wildebeest.

"We were still sleeping together," I said. "People don't sleep with people they hate."

"Well, that's not true," David said.

David was an aspiring screenwriter and my most reliable friend. I didn't tell him about my upcoming movie meeting. The mood of betrayal had gone general.

"Men like me," I said, hand on the belly that housed a being of unknown gender. "They really do. Just yesterday a man stopped me on the sidewalk to ask me if I was Italian."

"Who was talking about not liking you? You're just in pain."

"Maybe I'm not in pain."

"I'd put my money on pain. It's the Kantian sublime, what you're experiencing. There's your life, and then you get a glimpse of the vastness of the unknown all around that little itty-bitty island of the known."

Sublime. I thought of it as a flavor. Maybe related to key

lime. I didn't know what the Kantian sublime was. It's important to be an attentive host. And wife, for that matter. I went
to the kitchen and got out some crackers and mustard and
jam; it was what I had. I found some little decorative plates to
make it look nicer. Suddenly I was worried that David might
leave, that I'd have no company left in the world.

"You know who I get fan letters from?" I said. "I do get
fan letters. That's something, isn't it? Maybe there's a certain
distance from which I'm lovable. I get fan letters only from
men. Only from men in prison."

I set down the confused cracker offering.

"You really haven't looked at the blog?" David let the
crackers just sit there. "On the one hand, I want to congratu-
late you. But it might help you, to look."

I spread mustard on a cracker.

"I used to get fan letters from prisoners, too," David said.
"Back when I ghostwrote that column for *Hustler*."

"Are you competing with me?"

"I'm just sharing. This is intimacy, Trish."

"One of the letters I got was about love. It was like seven
pages long. Like a lengthy philosophical inquiry into the nature of love as written by a very smart fifteen-year-old. Not
sex, but love. He specified that, like, maybe seven times. Maybe
that means it was about sex. Anyhow. About love."

"What you're saying is somehow not becoming; you don't
sound like yourself."

Life, I was deciding, was a series of stumblings into the
Kantian sublime. Not that I knew one sublime from another,
as I said, but I planned on asking David about that when I was
feeling less vulnerable. "Well, this kid said he wanted to con-
firm with me some impressions about love that he had gotten
from my book. He wanted to know if I'd been honest about
what love was. He said he would one day get out of jail, and
that it was important that I write back to him. He said I could

take as long as I wanted to get back to him. 'As long as you need,' he said. 'You must be busy, take a year, that's fine.' "

"That's gracious, that he gave you an extension at the university of him."

"I thought it was sweet. I didn't write back."

"Did I tell you that the pilot thing is finally fully dead now?"

"Gosh."

"Do you miss Jonathan?"

"I wanted to tell you," I said, "about this other letter, too. I don't know why this guy wrote to me in particular. He didn't say. He was also a prisoner. He was very polite. He said simply that he had an idea for a movie, that it involved the Tunguska incident of 1908, and he wanted to know if it was a reasonable hypothesis that the explanation for the Tunguska incident could be antimatter—"

"I wonder if I would get a lot of work done if I was in prison—"

"I didn't know what the Tunguska incident was. I had to look it up. Turns out there was this place in Siberia where for thousands of acres the trees were suddenly laid flat. No scientists really bothered to check it out for years and years. But there were reports of unbearably loud sounds, apocalyptic winds, strange blue lights. It must have looked and sounded like the end of the world. They think maybe it was a meteor. Some people saw a column of blue light, nearly as bright as the sun, moving north to east. Some said the light wasn't moving, just hovering. Windows hundreds of miles away were broken."

David was reading aloud to me from Jonathan's blog as I went and got the printouts of witness accounts I had found on that horrible thing called the Web.

"See, it's not even really *you*," he was saying.

"Shhh," I said. "Listen." I read out: " 'The split in the sky grew larger, and the entire northern side was covered with fire. At that moment I became so hot that I couldn't bear it, as if my shirt were on fire, I wanted to tear off my shirt and toss it down, but then the sky shut closed, and a strong thump sounded, and I was thrown several yards—' "

"God, I would have loved to be there, that really was the sublime—"

"They say that for many nights afterward the sky over Asia and Europe was still bright enough to read the paper by."

"Did you answer the letter?"

"I told him I couldn't think of any reason why antimatter wasn't a plausible explanation. Though who was I to answer that question? I wished him luck with his idea. I might even have signed the note 'Love.' "

I lent David three hundred dollars, which seemed confirmation of my having taken advantage of him in some fashion.

Did I then take that movie meeting, all unprepared, after dressing in a way to accentuate my pregnancy, then to downplay it, then changing outfits again to accentuate it? Did I have no ideas? Did I start talking about the Kantian sublime, and about meteors and about love? A transgenerational love story with an old shepherd in Siberia, and a latter-day woman who knits, and a transfigurative event, and the sense that life is an enormous mystery but with secret connections that, you know, knit us all together? I did. All those things I so studiously knew nothing about. Meteors enter the Earth's atmosphere every day. I was betraying so many, I felt so clean.

REAL ESTATE

At first I'd thought nobody else was living there. It had been decided that selling the admittedly pretty run-down five-story town house would be easier if the place could be shown and delivered essentially vacant. That way the prospective buyer could "dream." The building's "good bones" would be made plain. It was a prime location, and a historic one! Maybe a former newsboys' orphanage, I could never remember. A buyer could make, say, two small income-generating apartments per floor; that would mean ten modest, easy-to-rent units for this down economy. Or luxury floor-throughs could be made. Or maybe the top two floors could be converted into an owner's duplex, and the rest made into tidy rental units that would cover expenses. A carriage house could be put up in the garden. The possibilities were endless. It was the ideal choice for someone with imagination! Architects could be recommended.

The building belonged to a distant aunt of mine, a wealthy can-do woman who lived on another continent. And seeing as I lived on this continent, and was in a cash state that left me without a strong opinion on the tax code, I did not decline my aunt's offer of living in the otherwise empty building, making myself available to show the place when opportunities arose, and just generally being there to make sure it was OK. I moved on in. The switch of neighborhoods was somehow reason enough for me to stop seeing any friends. I didn't sign up for cable, and so had neither Internet nor television. And the radio, I don't know, I've never liked it

At first it seemed a kind of happy decadence, to live like that. But I guess I got a bit out of sorts. I remember a mid-morning when I was regretting an outfit of a particular pair of jeans and a brash yellow sweater, and then, when I stepped out to get the mail, I realized I was in my undershirt and pajama shorts; I realized that I'd never put on the regrettable outfit in the first place. Another afternoon I found myself anxious about the upcoming election, but then, walking past a poster for a newly released action movie, I realized that no, it was March and not October, and the election had been decided months earlier. One Monday: I was under the impression that I had stocked the refrigerator with Armenian string cheese, too much of it, so much of it that I'd need to eat it at two meals a day for a full week in order to keep it from going to waste, and then I went to the refrigerator, I found no string cheese there at all, just a sack of apples that I thought I'd only contemplated buying but then hadn't. That was the day I met my neighbor, Eddy.

When he saw me there in the foyer, he startled. His hair was long and unwashed, and he was carrying *Being and Time*, which didn't immediately make me dislike him, maybe because I liked his hair and maybe because he carried it like it was a car repair manual. Actually maybe I startled first, before him.

I introduced myself as the niece of the landlady. I felt very nineteenth century doing that.

"Yeah, she's so nice," he said. "She's letting me stay in my place awhile longer."

I figured he was lying, but I also don't kick puppies. He went up the stairs. I went out the front door. Well, good, I thought. I'd been kind of spooked living in that building all alone. After that foyer meeting, when I'd hear all those noises that old buildings inevitably make, I would think, Oh, that

must be Eddy, opening his door, flipping a light switch, pour-
ing water over ramen noodles. Eddy looked through an old
photo album, opened seltzer cans, caressed a fussy and small
black cat I'd come to believe in. He creased pages in *Being and
Time*, the only book, in my mind, that he had. It wasn't exactly love, but it was better than the emotions that had pre-
ceded it. I'd rather not go into those emotions.

.

A week or so later I experienced a repeat of the phantom
string cheese episode. Except this time there was only one
apple left in the fridge, and it didn't look so great. I put on the
brash yellow sweater that I'd not yet had the chance to regret
in real life and ventured out. The string cheese mistake reprise
had given me a scare, and so I resolved to go farther than the
corner grocery. I needed to get out more, I decided. About
seven blocks away, I found a little family-run-looking gyro
place. I went on in, making the bells that hung on the handle
jingle as I did. The sound was as if somewhere an old-fashioned
filmstrip needed to be advanced.

At the back of the shop a man was pressing a waxed paper cup against the lever for a fountain Coke. I really love
fountain Coke. My whole family does. Maybe that's why I
found myself walking straight over there, to right next to that
man, to get myself a Coke—I could pay later, it seemed like
that kind of place—and then that man—something about the
tilt of his neck produced a tingle of recognition—mumbled
"goddammit" as foam ran over the edge of his soda cup. Memories ambushed me: endless rounds of gin rummy, my dad
drenched in sweat after a run wearing one of his button-up
work shirts, a track made up of old tires submerged in a field,
piles of pistachio shells. Sometimes I called up these little
father memories on purpose, but they weren't in the habit
of arriving unbeckoned. That neck, that "goddammit"—they

were familiar. But it couldn't be my father; he'd been dead for more than a dozen years, a baker's dozen, technically. But even if he'd been dead for just a day, it still would have been dead enough for it not to be him, there, cursing a soda machine.

I walked away from the soda machine, no soda in hand. I went casually about my business. I paid for my canned drink from the cooler, ordered a gyro, paid for that, too, waited, and then, with a filled red plastic basket in hand, I looked around for a seat.

He did look just like my dad. The way my dad looked thirteen years ago anyway. Not a day older. It was even kind of a good hair day for that man, and my dad always looked a bit younger when his hair was on the greasy side, and so a little darker, and that was how this man was looking, with his now mostly emptied wax cup of fountain Coke. He was seated at a corner table. He half smiled at me. Maybe I was staring.

He didn't say my name, or call me little cough drop, or numkin, or ask me how I was doing, or say It's been a long time, hasn't it? He just said to me, lightly, "You should sit here."

Spilled yogurt sauce on our table glistened as if refracting the grandeurs of the sunken city of Atlantis; stray salt crystals reflected fluorescence back at madcap angles. Or at least that was my mood. My father pawed some napkins, wiped his forehead with them; onions always made him sweat.

I asked him if he lived nearby.

"Sort of," he said. Then: "Not really." Then: "Not originally." He finished his meal quickly.

As he exited, those bells on the doorknob rang.

Had I slipped through a wormhole of time? An advertisement poster on the wall showed a blond woman with eighties bangs leaning in to take a bite of gyro while a caption offered pronunciation guidance. But it was hard to take "yee-ros" as evidence; all the gyro places I've ever visited have been outdated.

.

That night Eddy paced his apartment. A creaking that increased in pitch, then decreased. Increased, then decreased, like the breathing of an enormous man. He was wondering, I decided, whether he should come pay me a visit.

The next day I returned to the gyros place. When I walked in, that chain of bells jingled so beautifully. Much more beautifully than the day before. I thought of the underwater warbling of sirens. "It's nice to see you again," my dad called out across the narrow restaurant.

I ordered a beer with my lunch, which I never do. I got a Coke, too. My dad's hair didn't look quite as good as it had the day before. But when I asked for the yogurt sauce bottle and he passed it to me, I found myself thinking of the vast distances between nuclei and electrons, the tremendous nothingness of matter, the dizzying transformation of energy, and how magnificent a feat this was, my father passing the yogurt bottle. He was amazing. An amazing man. We were all amazing.

We got to talking about gin rummy, and I guess I invited the man over to play for a bit. We played for hours. What was weird was that it was very normal. And the whole building seemed happy. There was laughter in the stairwell, cloppity footsteps, old music playing; the lyrics to "Georgy Girl" by The Seekers made their way to me. Eddy was having a party? It was like real estate staging taken to another level; someone visiting would have felt impulsively moved to buy, I think. Although on some level all that "life" kind of creeped me out. An old friend of mine, Betsy, once told me a story of having roomed in a haunted house. What she meant by haunted house was that she had heard that everyone who had stayed there had been haunted. There'd once been a suicide, there was a thought that might be the ghost. Anyhow, Betsy was dreading the haunting. Which didn't arrive, didn't arrive, didn't arrive. Then one night it did. A doorknob rattling, pacing, a low moaning sound . . . the whole works.

But then that was it. Just that one visit, that one night. And Betsy thought, Ghost, why did you leave me? Have I done something right?

Next morning I noticed that the one clock in my place had stopped. It wasn't a fancy grandfather clock, or a charming old windup, or a pocket watch on an old brass chain. Just this little LED thing of mine, which has worked for years and years. Survived many a power surge, many a move. No more. I felt a little discouraged. But having no idea what time it was gave me a valid excuse to seek out Eddy. I could ask Eddy about the time. Just about that.

On the other side of Eddy's door I heard footsteps. I knocked. The footsteps abruptly stopped. "Eddy?" There was no answer. Was he worried I would complain about the noise from the party? "Eddy? It's just that my clock stopped working." Maybe he thought I was going to try to kiss him. Maybe that was his version of a nightmare. I knocked one more time. More nothing.

People have moods; that's certainly something I know firsthand. I try not to judge. I went back down the stairs. For a bit the quiet was, well, deafening, but after a while—obviously I don't know after how long—the pacing upstairs resumed. Other odd noises, too. Squeaks. A couple of chirrups. Something that sounded like newspapers being folded.

Eventually—the sun was still high—I walked out to the gyro place. Those bells jangled in a mediocre way when I entered. That soda fountain was there, also the smell of fresh-cut onions. I didn't recognize any of the patrons. I still haven't seen my father again. Nor have I seen Eddy. It's only been twenty-two weeks or so, though. And the other morning I thought there was string cheese in the refrigerator, and then there it was, actually there. Maybe it's wrong of me, but I do hope that nobody buys this building for a long time. I have the sense that ghosts like to return to the same places. I, anyhow, like to do that. And there is something about the bones of this place; it really is easier to dream here.

DEAN OF THE ARTS

I owe to the convergence of boredom and an atavistic attraction to the color gold the discovery on a near-empty shelf in my childhood home (and in my childhood) of *The Collected Correspondence of Manuel Macheko*. The only other books in the house offered health or income tax advice. But Macheko wrote to Menachem Begin, explaining that Begin's last name was confusing; to Barbara Bush, offering a broccoli recipe (with cumin seeds) that might persuade her husband to take "a new view of the humble crucifer"; to hair dye companies, seeking free samples of dyes they might recommend to men. His book had over me the kind of power more often attributed to a Vermeer: a room with a map on the wall, a letter just arrived, a ship on the sea visible through the window, and the window letting in light from a wondrous and unboundable world that would one day make its way to you, surely as the Annunciation. That was the feeling I got anyway. Back then. I didn't understand the letters as attempts, at least in part, at comedy. A surprising number of the pursued correspondents replied, sometimes tersely, sometimes expansively, and their responses were included in the book, alongside Macheko's original letters. In fact, the book was dedicated "To those who took the time to respond." Sometimes Macheko's sentiments were "appreciated" or "had received due consideration." But sometimes more. A former Indian prime minister had taken the time to handwrite an extensive note confirming that he did drink his own urine every day as part of his health regimen, which also included celibacy, and celery. Joan Rivers stated that she had not had a face-lift, just two and a half hours of ingenious hair and makeup. Helen Gurley Brown advised Manuel to just ask his girlfriend straight out if she had herpes.

I don't know how many copies of the self-published book existed, or exist. I believe Macheko distributed them himself. When I got older, I came to think of that book, for reasons I can (sort of) explain, as a cry for help. That said, not long ago I was looking at a handbook of facial expressions designed to teach autistic youth how to read emotion; it consisted of captioned photos of happy faces, of angry faces, of worried faces, etc; I couldn't really "read" the supposedly easy-for-normal-people-to-"read" faces; I mean, I could, but also I couldn't; I could tell what emotions I was *supposed* to see, sure, but to my heart, they all read the same, they all looked like cries for help.

•

Despite looking it up repeatedly, I seem never able to recall the name of the preacher of the sinners-in-the-hands-of-an-angry-God sermon, and I am similarly chronically unable to recall the real name of the pseudonymous Mr. Macheko. I retain only that he was a Persian—his term—professor living in Norman, Oklahoma (where I lived), and that when I came across his book, he had already been, or shortly thereafter was, fired from his position as a professor under circumstances that were, I was given to understand from my own father, a colleague of his, in some way unjust or superstitious or not unrelated to the author's having especially dark skin and a warbling accent and a mysterious religion in an almost entirely white—and oddly preppy—department of a university in one of the most politically conservative university towns in the country. I had once heard rumors, similar to those about the high school French teacher, that Macheko attended a weekly cross-dressing night at a bar in Oklahoma City. I think I instinctively understood, of both men, that the rumors were a version of slander that a patina of time and geographical shifting would reveal as a readiness for veneration, or fear, but not truth. But of the firing: presumably, Macheko was also straightforwardly irritating. That can cause anyone problems.

I mention this irritatingness in order to give the benefit of doubt, at least kind of, to the midwesterners I grew up among, who took me—also an odd-looking foreigner—into their homes, and who taught me more about openness and social justice than anyone since, and about whom no one around me these days is, I think, fair. And I presume this—that Macheko was irritating—because his son was one year ahead of me in high school and he played trumpet. He was very, very talkative. He had bad acne, a big nose, glasses, lots of energy, and a cheerfulness whose border none of us had encountered. The social shame heaped unjustly and unsurprisingly on young Macheko for reasons of genetics and origin and whatnot—he took that and steam-engined it into just more gregariousness and academic distinction. Even: our art teacher gave up Friday lessons to "Bible Jeopardy," and though it was not Macheko's sacred text—I think he was Zoroastrian—his team almost infallibly won. Lots of kids disliked young Macheko, and even more mocked him. Some went so far as to throw stones at him. Yet his exuberance only intensified. He had good things to say about everyone.

Once, for a weekend debate tournament, he and I were assigned to be partners, to be a team of two set to debate other teams of two. The debate topic was "A person has the right to die how and when he or she chooses." We had to argue both Affirmative and Negative. For Negative, we focused on what we decided was the overlooked "how" of the proposition; it was a silly argument—as if the issue were people's right to

kill themselves by stepping into the middle of a freeway or by
drowning themselves at a city pool—but a technically sound
one, and we won all four rounds that day, easily. We knew we
had to come up with a new set of rebuttals for what, by the
second day of the tournament, would be premeditated coun-
terarguments, and so late into the night, over fried okra and
many teas at the local diner, we worked out ideas and arguments, at first about the debate topic and then slipping toward this, that, and the mark of Cain. "Innocent Abel has no
descendants," Macheko-son said, as if someone had inquired.
"We forget that we're all descendants of Cain, not Abel. It's
like each of us wears the mark of Cain, like each of us has
killed our brother. And people think God marked Cain to
shame him, but that's not it." Still no one was inquiring but
he was responding. "The mark was to protect him. The mark
meant that anyone who punished Cain would be punished by
God sevenfold in return. It's not for us to judge!" Macheko
said. "Something like that." We moved on, to other topics.
Talking was easy. In some sense, we had a lot in common.
Then, at around one o'clock in the morning, I don't know
how to describe what happened except to say that young Macheko gave me a look. Not a romantic look; it was more awful
than that. He gave me a look that seemed to signal an immi-
nent confession of Machekovian isolation and misery. A confession that, if I heard it, would draw me into an obligation I
could not come even close to fulfilling. I would be a passing
meal for an eternally starving golem, and I would be nothing
else. "Whoa, I am so tired," I said. "Jesus. It's like somebody
just hit me over the head with a club." I left.

At the tournament the next day we lost the Negative
rounds and won the Affirmative ones. For the rest of high
school I avoided young Macheko, and I tried not to think of
him in the twenty years following. I did hear that he hadn't

had the means to leave town for college, but that eventually the Macheko family had moved away—to somewhere, or to a few somewheres. I myself had also left and not returned.

.

Then last year I was down in Mexico City for a couple of weeks. I was going through an intense bout of fearfulness that is too irrational and stupid and elusive to explain, and I had done what my husband termed pulling a geographical. I realize it isn't common to think of Mexico City as a haven from fear. Anyhow, there I could in conscience afford things I couldn't normally afford because life was cheaper but not so very much cheaper that one felt awful all the time (though one felt somewhat bad). I found myself getting a manicure and a pedicure, which was weird for me, I don't even like the look of manicured nails, and having a stranger attending to my cuticles with sharp and blunt objects: it just all feels very wrong. As I was engaged in this incorrectness, I found myself in conversation with a Mexican woman who was, she said, a television news reporter. Or rather, she used to be a television news reporter. Until she had gotten into a bad car accident. Followed by a long recovery period. She had become very depressed in that period and put on a lot of weight. Forty pounds! The television station told her that if she wanted to keep her job, she would need to take the weight off; they said they'd give her four months to do it. I was American, right? Oh, she knew my neighborhood in New York! because she had dated the grandson of Norman Mailer, and Norman Mailer had lived there, hitting on her, yes, even from his deathbed, no, that relationship had not worked out, neither the one with Norman Mailer nor with the grandson of Norman Mailer. She was soon going to be covering the Mexican midterm elections, if all went well with the diet. She might have to go to

Sinaloa, or Chihuahua, in any case to a place where the narco wars were very much alive. Her friend was in Juárez; he saw bodies in the streets. Well, that's the North!

The young woman handling my feet tenderly asked me what color I wanted my toenails painted. The TV reporter asked me what was I doing in Mexico City.

I wasn't feeling like myself, and the light was lumbering through the extra-thick window, bending into a bright diadem, which maybe explains how I found myself getting lime green toenails and saying I was writing a culture piece about Mexico City for a magazine. For *The New York Times Magazine*. I hadn't really figured out what I would focus on; I was a little lost, to be honest.

Except for the bit about being lost, what I'd said was not true. I'm a molecular biologist, for one thing. I study epigenetics, things that alter expression of the genetic code but that aren't themselves in the genetic code. It's actually pretty interesting, I think, but it's difficult to find a way to "chat" about it with strangers, it being difficult to chat about methylation and histones.

I know the perfect thing! the TV reporter said. You should write about me and my friends! She could show me a real circle of artists and writers. When she said circle—she had switched to speaking English; her colloquialisms were good—I thought for a moment she said circus. It sounds narcissistic, she laughed, but American readers would be very interested, and it would be very easy and fun for me, she explained, and it would really be a help to her, too, because she wanted to get a different kind of work, work in the U.S., work that she knew she'd be great at, and it was very difficult to live in Mexico just now; she loved Mexico, of course. There were enough negative stories about Mexico City, this would be a positive one! She just needed to lose a little more weight. And establish herself in the U.S. She was so lucky that she had met me. This was really going to be great.

I said that I, too, thought that sounded great.

I imagine that there are those who, even if it was misdirected, might at least briefly enjoy being an object upon which esteem and hope are projected. There are those who can be lighthearted about a basic deception and/or error and either correct it or just go with it and then even do whatever little thing they can do to give the people around them what they want or need and who can then handle whatever disappointment ensues. Some people might not find that even someone's minimal excitement about them provokes imaginings of that scene, which may or may not be in Dante but is certainly somewhere in my education, where the narrator is in some boat, crossing some river into the underworld, maybe the Styx, or Lethe, and the dead souls in the river are clamoring to get aboard, though of course they will not be able to get aboard, because they are the damned, whereas the narrator is still alive and not yet judged. When heading out to meet Annalise (that was her name) the next day, I might even have thought briefly of Manuel Macheko. Or at least of that gold-jacketed book, of those letters obliquely asking for help, and setting out on journeys from which news might or might not return.

Or maybe I didn't think of Macheko's book. Maybe it was only in retrospect that I thought of the Machekos.

·

I arrived at a crowded cantina in the Condesa neighborhood. People were gathered to watch Mexico versus France in the World Cup. "This is my great friend Alice!" Annalise said, introducing me around a table crowded with good-looking people, a number of them wearing glasses with "personality." She then followed up with further biographical details about

me, most untrue, some of which I was not even responsible
for having related to her. My name is not Alice, but to be fair,
I had told Annalise that it was. Someone at the table ran an art
gallery; someone was studying architecture at Yale; or maybe
his girlfriend was doing that, and he was in a rock band;
someone had on a very nice suit jacket over a seafoam-colored
shirt. The cantina was noisy with cheer and chatter. A corn
and cream snack showed up at the table, looking somehow
luxurious in little tumblers, with a sprinkle of hot pepper. A
round of mescal was ordered! A goal was scored! The cantina patrons stood up and cheered. Little kazoos were being
blown.

"The narcos don't want Mexico to win," the rock musi-
cian or architecture student explained to me. "It makes the
people confident. They start expecting things." The woman
next to him, who looked maybe one-quarter Indian and was
tiny, under five feet—this made her otherwise straightforward
beauty otherworldly—had recently finished an art project
called *Canned Laughter*, cans that said "laughter" on them.

"This is what Uribe did in Colombia," a drunk older man
said to me. "He killed every single one of them. Not just the
narcos, but anyone associated with the narcos. A narco accountant. A narco driver. A narco nephrologist. All of them.
You have to kill them all. Then you can let them come back,
slowly, because of course there will always be a narco business.
But you can't let them think they own the country."

"You can't just put them in jail?" I asked.

"Jail is like Club Med for them," he said. He had wide-set
brown eyes, and upon reflection, he was kind of handsome.
There were more drinks. I started not to mind whatever was
said, including "It's so important for people to know what's
what. I wrote a poem about it."

"It's so good that you can show how involved the arts are

here with the real world," Annalise said to me. "About the situations in which we produce, our means of production. I'm so, so happy that you're here." Even more snacks came to the table. I felt bad for Annalise, trying to lose weight in a drinking and snacking culture.

And not much later that was the end of it. That was the afternoon. Mexico won the game. I was drunk.

I took a long nap. In my dream, I walked into some sort of cantina or bar or pool hall or all of those things, and my father was there, though his face was that of my husband. I had two young boyfriends, or just young male companions, with me. The thing that was weird about my father's being there was that he is dead, and this was true even in the dream, and so what was he doing there, mobile and breathing? I went ahead and approached him, in the middle of his pool game. He had his own face now. "Why didn't you at least call to say you were still alive?" I asked. "At least a phone call. A letter. Something." He didn't really say much in return. In (dream) fact, he said nothing. Nor did my manifestation or questioning appear to startle or disturb him. His face—now it was my husband's face again—was pale, and he shrugged his shoulders and went back to his pool game. I wondered if he was mentally well. Then I called my mom and my sister, from a public telephone that was there in the bar, to tell them the news—that the head of our family was alive. They already knew; they had always known. Why hadn't they told me? "He was dead to us. We were hiding nothing."

I woke up not sweating, but very thirsty. I saw that my husband had called, but I didn't return the call.

·

Around 10:00 p.m., I arrived at another cantina. A smaller group was gathered. Annalise spotted me at the entrance, got

up from her seat, ran over to hug me, and also gave me three
cheek kisses. The physical affection made me feel compan-
ioned and safe in the world, even as in my heart I was supposedly very skeptical of her affection, or really, of late, anyone's
affection. And even as her affection was directed to a falsely
named and attributed me. The crowd was already rowdy. A
plate of limes was accidentally knocked over. I ordered just a
single beer; it arrived alongside a free shot of tequila. Someone was shouting angrily about peccaries. Or about Gregory
Peck movies? Someone patted my knee. Over the bar, a small
television was showing a rerun of the soccer match from earlier in the day. The patrons still cheered at the game's key moments, as if the game were live, its outcome unknown. I
cheered, too. Ordering another beer, I wondered about both
my own and Annalise's waistline. Perhaps this was the start
of a genuine empathy?

There was a three-man band—two large guitars, a wash-
board with an attached harmonica—that came by the table,
sang a corrido, took their tip, then went back to hanging
around closer to the bar itself, watching the tiny television.
When a new group of patrons arrived, the band went over to
them, not immediately, but soon enough, to play again.

I heard shouting at the entrance.

The entrance doors were saloon doors, though I hadn't
noticed that when I myself had entered.

Annalise ran up to a man there at the entrance. To stop
him? Was he angry? Dangerous? They kissed one another's
cheeks, maybe ten or fifteen times, although not like lovers, or
like former lovers, or like anything like that.

"You know who that is, right?" someone sitting near me
said.

"No," I said.

"That's Manuel Macheko," he said.

Or at least I heard him say Manuel Macheko. I felt sweaty,

DEAN OF THE ARTS   129

and afflicted by a ringing sound that no one else seemed to
register, and also as if someone I long trusted had revealed his
willingness to throw me to the dogs. Was it just the remnants
of my dream talking to me? Was I really haunted by Manuel
Macheko? "Who did you say that was?"

"You know, he was a great friend of bunuelos. And also
of monkey vice."

Or, again: I heard him say bunuelos and monkey vice. I
was pretty sure *bunuelos* was Spanish for "little doughnuts."
Then I realized, no, he had said Bolaño. I had at least heard of
Bolaño. As for Monkey Vice, I made no progress in rehearing
that into a more reasonable name. Instead, I just heard monkey vice, monkey vice, monkey vice. I was able to deduce that
this Monkey Vice was a relatively recently dead intellectual of
considerable stature. Who had loved cats. Someone very beloved. Whom everyone now wished they could say that they
had known well. It became obvious to me that I would seem
like a loser and perhaps a colonialist if I let on that I had no
idea about the venerable Monkey Vice, and only a dim rumored sense of Bolaño—these men who cast, even from their
graves, a glow upon the Manuel Macheko with whom Annalise was walking back to our table. Whose life was this? Not
mine.

"The name is Manuel Macheko?" I confirmed quietly with
the man on my right.

"Yes, yes, Manuel Macheko," he repeated.

Up close, this Macheko was an unusually short, ugly, and
joyous-looking man. I didn't recognize him. But I had never
met the father of the young Macheko. This Mexican Macheko
was not as dark as the young Macheko. I couldn't securely as-
sign any ethnicity to the man there before me, though I can
reliably say that I wouldn't have not believed the man in front
of me was native Mexican—probably mestizo—nor would I
have not believed that he was Persian. All I had as a compare

was a fallible memory of the cover of the Machekan correspondence book, in which the author had appeared as an
inked cartoon sketch of a man with a small mustache, sitting
at a typewriter with an unfurling paper scroll upon which
could be made out the names of well-knowns. Not very
pathognomonic. And why had I never before wondered why a
Persian man had taken a Hispanic pseudonym?

"To see him alive is always like a miracle," Annalise whispered into my ear. Macheko was standing and shouting at the
little television with a raised fist. The coach of the Mexican
team is a Communist! He only plays the old broken-down
players! He's punishing the young stars for their big contracts
in Europe! Mexico would never go far with this asshole making decisions! Then, fatigued, Macheko sat down. I couldn't
tell if he was familiar with the result of the game or not. The
musicians came by. He tipped them well and requested what
proved to be a very short song. A candy vendor came by; Macheko bought a pack of mint gum from him, offered it around
the table, then put it in his pocket, having taken none. In a
more rapid Spanish than usual, which I couldn't follow so
well, Annalise introduced Macheko to me. She called me a
brilliant journalist, I think. Macheko kissed my face several
times.

I wanted to ask him if he had ever taught at the University
of Oklahoma or if he had a son who played trumpet. Alice,
however, did not want to ask. And I was Alice.

Macheko ordered a round of beers for the table, each one
of which again came with a shot of tequila. He was reillumi-
nated as he spoke to me. There was some notion in the air
that I could be of tremendous help, though again I couldn't
really follow; the cantina had only become noisier and more
crowded. Macheko had written an account about a headless
something? Why it hadn't yet been translated into English

was just for some fucking reason and because people were cowards?

I said: Didn't you write some sort of set of letters? Letters in English?

He simultaneously ignored me and kept speaking to me. He could do the English translation himself! They wouldn't even have to pay a translator! Fuck his other projects, this was his most important work! Macheko's Spanish sounded less Mexican, more something else that I couldn't place, but I'm not in truth so very good at placing accents. I once asked Germans if they were Canadians. We were interrupted by a man wearing what looked like an accordion connected to what looked like two ends of jump rope with metal handles. Macheko talked the man down from thirty to twenty pesos. Then he stood up, took hold of the handles, and flexed his upper body in what appeared to be agony. This went on for what seemed to me like a long time, though probably it was less than ten seconds. The contraption was an electric shock machine. Macheko declared he felt much more awake now, much better.

"Take, take, you're welcome to it," Macheko then said, bringing out handfuls of little plastic bags of white powder and throwing them onto the table. "It's also a good way to wake up." He left the bags there as he headed to saloon-doored bathrooms in the back.

A man on my right explained to me that Mexico City had very clean, very inexpensive cocaine because everything passed through there, did I know that?

Upon his return, Macheko said to me that it was so wonderful that I was in Mexico, that I was obviously a good woman.

I did feel that he was staring at me with a kind of intimacy that exceeded the situation. Maybe he stared at me with

recognition. Or with a desire to be recognized? Could he see
my father's face in mine? Maybe his look was a petition of
some sort. A cry for help?

Then he said he had to go, and he was gone.

.

I stayed on awhile, past the end of the replay of the soccer
game. You have to help him, Annalise said. He has a metal
plate in his head. Another table member nodded in agreement.
It was communicated to me that Macheko was the guy who had
investigated those hundreds of murders of women in Juárez.
Who else had the courage to do that? He was the guy who said
to Monkey Vice: It's not a serial killer. Not a serial killer, but
part of the sick culture there. It was from him that Bolaño took
the famous line in his novel, the one where the woman says,
"¡No somos putas, somos obreras!" We're not whores, we're
workers! Someone said there were narco kids who thought it
was a laugh, or maybe it was an initiation, to shoot a woman
in the head while fucking her in the ass, for a special sensa-
tion. It needed to be widely known. The metal plate was mentioned again. It was something to do with some time when
Macheko was beaten to the edge of his life, left for dead.

I knew it was wrong that I judged these people, mostly
negatively, for being both fashionable and emanating flashily
unflashy wealth and being interested in "real" life—but it was
also real!—in this way; Macheko, the trumpeter and debater,
was telling me across the years that there was no place for
judgment, not of any kind. Is Macheko from around here? I
asked. Oh, he had lived everywhere. He had even lived in
Texas, someone said, but something had gone wrong with his
green card. Macheko had a secret hideout in his home; the
hideout was wall-to-wall books; it could be the home of
Edward Said, that was the quality of the books; you could live

there for a hundred years. He does so much work! He won't
survive if he stays here. Eventually they'll decide to get him.
You can help him, I was being told. You're the one who can.
You'll bring attention to him. Then he'll get his work pub-
lished in English. They'll celebrate him as a hero; they'll give
him a job and a green card and everything. That was the power
of those American magazines. They already love Bolaño in
America. They respect Monkey Vice. You should go north with
him. You can report on his reporting. It can definitely work.
Alice, you can make this happen.

   Alice said, Yes, you're right. It's important, I'll do whatever I can.

                                  •

Back in my plain-walled Mexican room, I tried to search for
the person I had encountered. My initial Internet searching
yielded no Machekos teaching in a chemical engineering department, which was the department from which the corre-
sponder had been fired. I did find a soccer player with the
name. Also an empty LinkedIn profile. Not only am I an in-
effective Internet searcher, but clicking through a few pages
on the Internet makes me feel as if I haven't slept for days. My
husband is immeasurably better at such things.

   It was three o'clock in the morning. I called him.

   To my joy and surprise, he answered.

   I explained about the original Macheko book. Then I described, in a limited way, this other Macheko—some Mexican
journalist, I said.

   "I'm looking," he said. My husband couldn't find Macheko books of any kind. But then, no, he found a copy of the
self-published correspondence book on a used books site. It
was listed for ninety-one dollars.

   I asked if there weren't any other books by the same writer?

Or a writer with a similarly spelled name? Had he looked, specifically, for books written in Spanish as well?

"Don't you think," my husband said, "that this being what makes you pick up the phone is a little bizarre? You basically vanish, you don't explain yourself, we don't know when you're coming back, and then, when you do call—"

I thought for a moment to ask after our daughter at that point, but I knew that would just seem defensive, probably even be defensive, seeing as I felt pretty sure about how she was doing; children, I remember this from my own experience, are, I think, very resilient and flexible, and one shouldn't let people tell one otherwise.

"I'm sorry," I said. "I guess I panicked."

"It's not just me you should talk to," he said.

"I get it," I said.

"You must get it and then forget it."

"I can only panic so many times. It's not fair to you."

"It's not really about fair or not fair. I need you. I really do. But eventually my body will figure it out, that it's no good to need you, and then I won't need you anymore. It'll be like a terrible cure."

I didn't have anything to say to that.

After some quiet, maybe with or without shuffling, he said, "You know what I can do for you? I can contact the seller. There's a way to do that. Who knows, maybe pz21147 can answer all your questions. Do you want me to contact him?"

I said that yes, I would really appreciate that. I said, "They have this thing here, these orange slices that they serve with paprika; it's really tasty; I'll prepare it for you when I come back."

"I'm tired," he said.

One of the more frustrating traits of my husband was how well he understood me. I had long thought of Macheko as someone seeking contact. But maybe not. Maybe those letters were part of building a hermitage. Maybe Macheko wrote to glittering strangers not with the unreasonable hope that they would see and know him but, rather, with the really quite reasonable hope that he would make contact with people who would almost certainly *not* know or truly see him, even if they did respond. I understand how that might appeal. I remember when I discovered that my father had kept secret from us years of working at a campus suicide hotline. He was always late coming home on Tuesdays and Thursdays, and one day I saw his car parked and went and investigated. I kept his secret a secret. I accustomed myself to the idea of my dad's listening to girls at slumber parties prank calling, and to lonelies who had lost jobs and lovers, and to those energetic people who must have abused him as heartless if he suggested that they visit an emergency room or accept an appointment to see a therapist the next day. I later also learned that my dad offered free tax advice for the poor in a booth set up every spring outside the Wal-Mart. He helped get green cards for students from China who really had no relationship to his field. I had known none of this. After he died, I found among his papers all sorts of elaborate thank-you letters he had received. Also a grievance list, by him, of ways he had been misunderstood and underappreciated by us, his family. Most of his complaints seemed valid; we had criticized him for eating more than his share of a bowl of almonds set out as a snack at a neighbor's dinner, for example. In person, my dad could barely make eye contact, and took his dinner while watching PBS at high volume in the living room. But I remember going to the Denny's with him once and the waitress there calling him by his first name and putting unasked-for whipped cream and strawberry sauce on my waffle. The approval and gratitude of near-strangers can be a kind of drug; or maybe it's fair to use the term "medicine."

Anyhow, there were four more days of Annalise and her

crowd. Annalise had a sick mother to support. The architecture student confessed to a fear of being kidnapped a second time. Macheko did not re-surface; no one was sure of his whereabouts. Maybe he had gone back north. Alice eventually flew back home and was not heard from again. I judged her, but I also told myself that I shouldn't judge; I said to myself that Macheko's friends could put together a Wikipedia page for him on their own, if attention was what was needed. I continued with my more objective researches. Pz21147 turned out to be a bookseller in Springfield, Missouri, whose books were priced by an algorithm, and who knew nothing about the origins of his copy of *The Collected Correspondence*.

.

About a year after the Mexico episode, I learned something of the fate of the original young Macheko. The wife of a colleague of mine met him. In fact, she worked under him. Young Macheko, it turned out, had gone to graduate school in music at Juilliard. For trumpet. He had married a woman who sang opera; on weekends he rode long distances on his motorcycle; he was the energetic new dean of the arts at the university where this wife of my colleague taught.

These were happy-sounding details; I recognized young Macheko's metabolism in them even if the particulars surprised me. "He's a great guy," I was told. "He's one of those makes-things-happen people. Maybe a little Teflon-y, sure, like you never feel like you can make genuine contact. But fun. And generous. He says to say hi. I told him maybe we could all get together. He was a little weird about that. He told me an interesting story, though."

In the eleventh grade the English classes at our high school spent three weeks studying Ralph Ellison's *Invisible Man*. Ellison is said to have been aloof toward aspiring black artists and intellectuals, and to have been charming with and

beloved among whites. That's what they say. Ellison was from
Oklahoma, from a town not far from where Macheko and I
grew up. Ellison's father worked delivering ice, and died from
a work accident—impaled on a cleaved ice shard—when Ellison
was just three. His mother then worked a miscellany of jobs,
of which little Ellison was ashamed. The "battle royal" scene
near the opening of *Invisible Man*, in which the young black
boys are set up to fight one another blindfolded in order to
entertain a gathering of white community leaders who are giving them small scholarships, is roughly autobiographical. At
eighteen Ellison jumped a freight train to Alabama to attend
Tuskegee University, where he was a music major and played
trumpet. In later life Ellison became nostalgic for his home
state. Turn of the century Oklahoma—Ellison's Oklahoma—
had at least twenty-eight all-black towns, with their own
newspapers and schools, and many of those communities
were prosperous. Those towns have since vanished; when a
book of Oklahoma ghost towns was put out, those towns
were absent even from that book. Shortly before Ralph Ellison
himself died, young Macheko, having just studied *Invisible
Man*, went to the public library, took out a New York City
phone book, and found a listing for "Ellison, R." He called. A
woman answered. The sixteen-year-old asked to speak with
Mr. Ellison. She said to hold on a moment. Macheko and
Ellison then spoke for more than two hours. About all the
things they had in common.

I admired Macheko-son. He had improved upon his
father's methodology. That was a tribute. I was not honoring
my line as well.

THE LATE NOVELS
OF GENE HACKMAN

Most of the presenters at the conference in Key West were somewhat old, and the audience was very old, which was something J was accustomed to, being among people considerably older than herself, since it is the older people, generally, who have money, and who thus support the younger people, who have youth. Or something. The young have something to offer. J had accepted the invitation to the seminars impulsively, in the middle of a cold February, because it promised a warm idyll for the following January, and because she was promised a "plus one." When the time came, months later, to choose the plus one, J invited not her gentle husband but her stepmother, Q, to join her. Q's latest business venture, an online Vitamins Hall of Fame, had failed. Also, Q's hair, which into her sixties had been a shiny Asian black—Q was Burmese—had begun to gray, and when she had dyed it at home, it hadn't gone back to black but had instead turned a kind of red. J thought that this sounded like no big deal, but it was apparently very distressing to Q. Same with the slightly below-normal results from a bone-density scan. "Do, you think when someone sees me on the street, they think to themselves, There goes an old woman?" Q asked.

"No," J said. This was on the phone. "I doubt they think anything at all." Then J felt bad for saying that. That was when she impulsively invited Q to go down to Key West with her the following January. J lived in Pittsburgh and Q lived

near Cleveland, so their communication lacked for enlighten-
ing facial expressions. J had recently e-mailed Q, jokingly,
about its being an ideal time to invest in Greek yogurt. Q wrote
back, saying that she'd bought ten thousand shares of Groupon's IPO. J couldn't imagine where Q had got the money.
After the initial offering, Groupon's shares sank dramatically.
It was rumored that there might have been fraud, insider
information—why had Q thought that she could swim with
sharks?! But Q hadn't purchased shares; she had just been
joking; Q seemed upset that J had even briefly believed she
had purchased Groupon shares. Only a sucker would do such
a thing. Did J really think she was such a sucker? Was that
what she thought?

J would definitely pack reading for their week together.

·

At the airport in Key West, J and Q were to be picked up by
M, who was somewhat old, or old on paper and not old in
person, or young, and who was one of the heads of the event.
Though J had never met M, she had been informed that M's
wife, who had been quite young, or younger, had not that
long ago died. Of something. One of the young-woman can-
cers was the impression she had. They had only just got married when the diagnosis came. Also, J knew that M wore an
eye patch. The eye patch was from an injury years earlier that
involved a champagne cork launched haphazardly by a third
party, unnamed, and surely still feeling guilty. "Please don't
stare at the eye patch," J instructed Q. "I'm telling you about
it in advance, so that you don't stare."

"I would never stare at an eye patch," Q said.

They exited from the plane directly into the outdoors and
then proceeded from sunshine into the small terminal building for baggage claim. Above the airport entrance gate there
were full-color, life-size statues of tourists or immigrants or

both, a crowd of them, with sculpted suitcases, gathered
together, in greeting or suffering; the statues resembled somewhat melted Peeps marshmallow candies. J and Q walked under them and into a tiny airport lobby. There was M! The
eye patch made him easy to spot. "Everything good?" he
asked. Yes, yes. "And you're—" He extended his hand to Q,
who said that she was Q, which didn't clear up much, but
enough. They headed out to the parking lot, to the surprise of
a little green convertible MG.

It was a sunny afternoon, and the wide road went along
sandy beaches at the soft water's edge. Just driving this little
car, ideal for two, must be traumatically lonely for him, J found
herself thinking. Sorrow's black wing now shades his brow,
she thought, as they proceeded at twenty-five miles an hour
on the quiet shoreline road, past occasional seagulls and the
foam of gentle waves. J was riding shotgun. Q was in the tiny
back, digging between the cushions in search of a seat belt
buckle that was not to be found. M was smiling. He was a
prominent popular historian. He chatted to J about the upcoming events, where dinner was that evening, what the expected weather was, who had already arrived, the various places
people were staying—

"You must feel like a bride," J said.

"A what?" M said.

"Like a bride," J repeated.

"Bride? Hmm. Well. No. I don't feel like a bride. What do
you mean?"

J felt obliged to stand by the tenuous comparison. "You
know: all this planning, now it's happening."

"I see. Well. No," M repeated. "I don't feel like a bride. I
don't really do much of the organizing. We have staff that
does that. My position is mostly honorary."

"Of course . . ."

"I just send a few initial e-mails to get things started. I

don't do the real work. It's just that I live here. Many of us have lived here, part-time, for decades. It's very nice, you'll see."

"Wait, why is he supposed to feel like a bride?" Q called out from the backseat.

"Not like a bride!" J corrected. "I was wrong about that."

M dropped J and Q off at their hotel, Secret Paradise, and said that he'd look forward to seeing them at dinner. J avoided saying what for some reason came brightly to mind: God willing.

.

The clock read 2:22 p.m. Their accommodation had a spacious bedroom, living room, kitchen, and luxury shower, in addition to a large private deck. Instead of the blank feel of a modern hotel room it had the eccentric collectible-salt-shakers-and-wicker atmosphere of a specific personality. "I could never live in this kind of a place," Q said. "With so many things on the wall and on the tables. I mean, it's nice. But it's very American."

J didn't like the decor, either, but she said, "Well, we are in America. Sort of."

"That man who picked us up didn't look like a writer," Q continued. "He was so tall. Like a lawyer, or a nice businessman."

"He's more a historian."

"A writer looks more like—there was that nice dog cleaner, remember? The guy who wrote poetry and did at-home dog cleaning? You remember, he had that van and would come to the house, and he would clean Puffin just there in the driveway. It was an excellent business idea that he had."

J was unpacking her things. "With animals it's called grooming, not cleaning. Cleaning is for carpets."

Q lay on the sofa and turned the television to the Weather Channel. J went out onto the deck. A wooden fence suspended on posts a foot or so off the sand blocked the view of the ocean, which was odd, though it did offer privacy.

J opened to the beginning of her book, which investigated the disappearance, in 1938, of Ettore Majorana, an Italian particle physicist. Majorana's disappearance might have been an escape, or might have been a suicide, or might have been a murder by Mussolini's government, or might have been something else. Majorana had for years behaved strangely: he didn't want to publish his work, or cut his hair, or see people—including his mother—whom he had previously enjoyed seeing. He may have been paranoid, or merely depressed. His work might or might not have been relevant to research into developing an atomic bomb. The historical moment made internal states that would normally be deranged—anxiety, grandiosity—seem quite possibly reasonable. Whatever the case, Majorana withdrew all the money from his bank account, boarded a boat to Palermo, and sent an apologetic goodbye-forever telegram to his employer, another telegram to his family, asking that they not wear black, then a further telegram to his employer, saying that in fact he would be returning—that he hadn't meant to be dramatic or like an Ibsen heroine, that he would explain it all on his return, a return that never occurred.

The book J was reading had been written in the 1970s by a Sicilian novelist who was famous, apparently, and had most often written about the Mafia. J looked over to the sofa where Q had lain down, but she could see only the sofa's back. For a moment, J felt certain that Q was gone. J walked over to the sofa; Q was there.

J's father had married Q two years after J's mother had died. J couldn't really remember her mother, though she had one vivid and most likely fabricated-from-a-photo memory of eating a frosted doughnut with sprinkles with her at a Winchell's when she was three or maybe four. J still loved doughnuts; Q had bought them for her every weekend morning. J and her sister were both blond and blue-eyed, and Q had often been mistaken for the girls' nanny. "Let people think their thinks" was a Q motto. When J's father had died, three years earlier, he had left Q a house and a teachers' union pension fund that must have been worth something, and Q had sold the house—not that she told the girls that she had done this—and moved into a small but tidy apartment. Q still worked part-time as a backup receptionist at a law firm, so there must have been some money left over, but it seemed possible that the money had been lost. Or, maybe, anxiously piled high in a savings account somewhere that she wouldn't touch. Or maybe loaned out irretrievably to distant Burmese cousins with unfortunate or naive investment strategies. That kind of thing had happened before with Q. When the sisters recently visited Q, she announced on the first evening that she had stopped ordering takeout, saying that it was for spoiled people. Maybe Q had bought the Groupon shares after all? And on margin? One never knew with Q. One day J had idly opened Q's passport, and it turned out that Q was eleven years older than she had been letting on for all those years.

·

"Your sister tells me Q has been staying at Morris's place," J's husband said. This was on the phone, around five o'clock, when J had stepped out to look for a lemonade she never found. Key West was humid and sleepy and closed. "Staying there while Morris is in the ICU with some sort of bad pneumonia." Morris was a retired accountant who had been in the same community choir as Q.

"She's probably just keeping the place cheerful and clean. Collecting the newspaper."

"Maybe. Or maybe she doesn't have her own place anymore."

"Illusion of trouble," J said, cheered that the conversation was moving her to the square of reason, since J's husband had made a knight's move to the square of paranoia.

As they talked, J found herself picturing their steep driveway, the cleavages of snow, a pile of the neighbor's discarded shingles waiting for pickup. And then it was "I love you, angel, I love you so much, OK?"

J felt scared. They were getting off the phone. One was supposed to be content and complete on one's own, to need nothing, and from that position one could truly give love— something like that.

·

When J returned to the room, Q said, "I think I won't come to the dinner."

"Why not?" J asked, alarmed.

"Maybe you don't want me there," Q said.

"But I do. It's a bunch of people I'm supposed to be collegial with, which is stressful. I don't want to go alone," J said, mostly truthfully.

"But I should lose weight," Q said. "I shouldn't go until I lose weight."

"You look nice. Plus, you don't even know these people."

"Even more so."

"The people who are thinner than you will be happy to feel relatively thin; the people who are larger, well, they'll be thinking about themselves. Actually, almost everyone will be thinking about themselves. You taught me that. Now I finally believe you. Just come. I suspect the food will be good."

The dinner was held in a large art deco home that J couldn't help but estimate as being worth around $2.2 million. Greeters—professionals wearing tidy black-and-white outfits—were in place at the entrance to an inner courtyard, and in addition to greeting they were warning guests that the house had many "tripping hazards." "Please be careful. There are a lot of steps that you might not notice," one of the greeters clarified. "We've marked them with red tape." It was true: there was a step down to a living room. A step up to a dining room. A couple of steps down to the porch. Steps back up to other rooms. Everything had its level. The backyard, which featured an artificial stream, crossable by a small footbridge, had tables set up for about a hundred guests, maybe more. The party was already crowded when J and Q arrived. Is Twitter like the ancient arcades or is it the end of literature? someone was asking. Someone else was explaining that his younger brother, after their bohemian upbringing in the Oregon woods and then having lived for years on boats, had run off with an evangelical musical theater project called Up with People. Reverse rebellion. What could you do?

J didn't manage to start up a conversation with anyone. She saw Q speaking with the hostess, with some intensity; M was also there, listening. Q was holding a drink. She looked as if she was enjoying herself. The hostess was wearing an aquamarine leather jacket that had slashes in the back, exposing an underlying black leather in a way that made J think of deboning a fish. The meal was grilled salmon on a quinoa salad, and also greens.

At the table: "It's so good to have a break," Q said to a prominent science fiction writer sitting near her and J. "Too many of my friends are sick or in the hospital."

"In the hospital for what?" a well-regarded older feminist who knew a lot about birds asked.

"Who's in the hospital?" M asked.

Q seemed to have the attention of the whole table.

"My friend was driving to the airport," Q said. "He was going to fly to the Philippines and then he couldn't turn his head, so he drove straight to the emergency room of the nearest hospital. Of course they just left him on a stretcher in the hallway for two days. They wouldn't have cared if he died— they did nothing for him. That's America for you. But then his friend arranged a transfer to another hospital. And at the second hospital they scanned him, and they found he had a big tumor in his neck. Also, he was missing one of his, I can't think of the word—"

"You write about medicine?"

"No, no, I just write e-mails," Q said. "I'm not a writer. But I was married to J's father—that's how I'm connected to J. J says I write very good e-mails."

"I woke up with my neck sore like that once," another science fiction writer said. In addition to writing, he was in a band that had a hit song based on *Beowulf*. "I didn't go to the hospital, though. I just took ibuprofen."

"But you *could* have gone to the hospital," Q said. "Because you all have insurance in England. The whole country is insured."

Now J was worried that Q didn't have health insurance; that was how her secrets usually manifested, like a tuba sound straying into a pop song. J intervened. "It wasn't just painful to move his neck. I think he really couldn't move it," she argued, as if Q were beleaguered, when in fact she seemed aglow. Also, J was just guessing at these details; she didn't know who or what Q was talking about.

"They have names like C2, C3," Q was explaining. "One of those Cs—he was missing it entirely."

"It had eroded away?" M asked.

"No, they just didn't know where it had gone," Q said. "I think maybe it was never there. I visited him after he had the surgery," Q went on. "They didn't remove the tumor because it was in a bad place for removing it, but they did give him an extra C made out of concrete—"

"I doubt it was concrete—"

"When I left to come down here, he was still in the hospital because he was afraid to go home until he had the results back from the biopsy. But I think he'll be fine. They scanned the rest of his body and found there were tumors in other places, too, which is a good sign—"

"That sounds like a bad sign," the woman knowledgeable about birds said.

"It's not a bad sign," Q said definitively. "I have a friend who's a doctor." Now Q seemed not aglow; she began to speak more slowly. "She says that after a certain age, if we look at anyone's body, there's all sorts of things there. When there's many things like that, it's not a problem."

"Incidentalomas," M said. "That's what you're trying to say. That lots of things are just incidentalomas. I agree completely."

"Has anyone seen that George Clooney movie that's playing?" J said. She ate quickly. J and Q weren't the very first to leave, but they were nearly the first, though they were detained near one of the tripping hazards as a very elderly and apparently blind man, dressed in an all-white suit and holding a cane, was being guided out by the greeters.

As he was passing, J asked, "Q, is there something medical going on with you?"

"I'm livelier than you are," Q said. "I could stay another hour, easy."

"I mean, do you have medical news?"

"You should be more cheerful," Q said. "It would be good for your health. You know—that would be something good to write about. About how you take on a good mood in order to have good health. You do that for thirty days and track what happens. That's something that would really sell. I mean, I admire that you tell stories of make-believe people in worlds that don't exist and that have no relevance to how we live. That can be nice, but people also like things that are up-lifting and practical."

•

The next day they were out the door by 8:19 a.m. There were almost no obligations; it wasn't until the following afternoon that J was expected to give a brief talk—on Martian dys-topias—and later have an also brief conversation. Her only other duty was to enjoy. And there was even a small stipend.

J and Q looked for somewhere to have breakfast. At the first café, omelets were $13.95, which seemed a little bit much. Not a lot much, but it just seemed unpleasant and like it would set expectations that the omelet really would be quite good, which surely it wouldn't be. It was already hot outside. At the next place, the omelet was $16.95. They went back to the first spot, where a window seat was available.

"I feel skinny in this town," Q said. "At least there's that."

It was true: although the festival participants were rela-tively fit, the locals were relatively not fit. And a bit flush in the face. Like alcoholics. Obviously they also had less money. One felt guilty noticing. Apparently the locals were called Bubbas. Why did everyone, even J and Q, feel superior to the Bubbas? It was terrible.

"And I think for a time, supposedly, this was a fashionable town," J said. "Artists and gay people. Which are both groups that I think of as made up of mostly thin people. And maybe a few charismatically fat ones."

"It's never charismatic to be fat," Q said.

"It can be, I think."

"No, never," Q said. "And there are no children here, either," Q observed. "That's the other weird thing."

J of course had no children, not yet, anyhow. Neither did Q—no "natural" ones.

"It's very weird," Q said, "to not have children. People who never have children are always still children, which, if you ask me, becomes disgusting. Even though children, of course, are sweet. I think the people who live here—I think they must have come here to run away from other things."

J had of late turned over in her mind the idea of having a baby that Q might move in to help raise; maybe Q needed a place to stay? "How's your friend Morris doing these days?" J asked. "I heard he was in the ICU."

"I think he's better," Q said. "To be honest, I didn't like visiting him in the hospital. I really thought he was dead. It was unpleasant."

"Who's taking care of his place while he's in the hospital?"

"Maybe his children? Though they're very selfish. Morris said over three hundred people visited him while he was in the hospital. That's because of his activity with the Toastmasters Club. It's really about being friendly and taking care of other people by cheering them up."

The omelet was not that good, though it wasn't bad. There was a newspaper.

"It says here that Gene Hackman was hit by a truck," J said. "He lives here. He was on his bicycle, and he was hit. Not very far from here at all."

"Is he OK?"

"It doesn't say."

"Is he old?"

"It says eighty-one."

"These days that's young. I bet he'll turn out to be fine."

Why would he be fine? J thought. It was a truck. He was eighty-one. The physics was not promising.

.

Twenty-four hours then passed in an extraordinarily slow blink. It was too hot to read or think or get hungry, and it wasn't even that hot. One could walk around, but there wasn't much territory to cover. The local graveyard was probably the prettiest thing in town. The graves were aboveground because the ground wasn't really ground; it was hard coral that could not be dug up. The graveyard didn't really look all that much like a graveyard; it was more like an ambitious papier-mâché project that schoolchildren had put together. Except that one saw no children. One saw lots of margarita bars. There was a party for a ninety-five-year-old art collector—maybe the blind man in white?—who owned many things in town, but J and Q slept through it. Finally it was the next afternoon, and J did an unusually bad job with her minimal obligations.

"You should have just told some jokes or something. Everyone likes to laugh," Q said. "We all need a little more laughter in our lives."

"I failed," J said.

"Sometimes failing is what's needed. I think it can put people in a good mood, to see someone fail. Let people entertain themselves. I think that's one of the reasons people are so lonely in this country. Because they always have to rush out and have someone else in the room entertain them. It's terrible, the loneliness here. People live in coffins. Like Morris—if it weren't for the Toastmasters, Morris would be in his coffin."

.

That evening there was a double birthday celebration for two people named Norm. The Norms! Turning seventy-five and eighty-five. J and Q didn't sleep through the party; they rode rented bicycles over to it. There were many loud-print shirts, and lots of alcohol. A woman with thick, long gray hair held back by a headband was wearing a high-waisted bright yellow skirt and platform sandals. Among the snacks were bright yellow peppers. The party was mostly outdoors, on a spacious deck between the main house and a guesthouse. Gentle lighting illuminated a small swimming pool. A little baobab tree grew through a hole in the deck. What might have been an anti-mosquito device had black light properties, or, at least, there was a pale blue Gatorade sort of drink that glowed in its aura, like new sneakers in a haunted house.

J found herself in conversation with a woman whose mouth dragged left, perhaps from a stroke, or maybe it was just a thing. The woman was a host, it turned out. It was her house; one of the Norms was her husband—her husband who was younger than her. The other Norm was staying in host Norm's guesthouse with his young lover, although apparently his young lover was, just for this week, staying elsewhere for half the time, because *his* even younger lover, "the chestnut," a graduate student in French literature, was in town, visiting. Visiting all of them. J realized that the host was the woman who had written a book called *Real Humans*, which J had for years been pretending to have read; it was a seminal nine-hundred-plus page post-apocalyptic book that imagined another way to live decently, ethically. On an island that, it was speculated, was modeled on Tasmania; there were creatures like wallabies there. J commented on how nice the guesthouse looked.

"Yes, we built that so our kids can stay there when they visit us. With their kids."

"That sounds smart," J said.

"Do you have kids?" the author of *Real Humans* asked.

"I don't," J said.

She looked J over. "Well, one day you will," she said. "What you'll find out then is that you don't like to cook breakfast for them. People are weird with their breakfasts. They have very particular demands, and you'll find that dealing with them can be very annoying."

"I can imagine," J said.

"You know what's strange?" the woman asked.

"OK. What's strange?" J wondered where Q was.

"You're going to go on living," she said. "And I'm not going to go on living. I might go on for a while. I'm eighty-seven. But you're going to continue into a future that I'm never going to see and that I can't even imagine. I mean, this cocktail party is just like one my parents might have thrown fifty years ago. But in other ways it's a completely different world. I hear people on their cell phones saying, 'Yes, I'm on the bus now. I'll be there in ten minutes.' Or, 'I'm in the cereal aisle now.' Well, that's just so strange to me. It's like people can't be alone. I don't find that normal. Do you find that normal? Do you do that tweeting? Do you understand those things? I know that I can't follow. So I just don't. But you're just going forward into the future. You'll go forward and forward, into it. And I won't."

"I'm here with my mom," J said. "I better go check in with my mom." J couldn't recall ever having used that phrase out loud. It sounded almost like science fiction.

She couldn't find her!

Then she found her.

Q was in conversation with M. And also with the lover of the other Norm, the guesthouse Norm. And also with a man who had lived for a long time on a boat. The man had lived on the boat when real estate in Key West was too expensive, he was explaining, but now he was back on the island again. Which had he liked more? Well, he liked both. Then the other Norm's lover was explaining that sure, Norm didn't like to sleep alone when "the chestnut" was in town. Especially since his recent health scare. But one couldn't be at the sugar teat all the time, the lover was of the opinion. The other Norm was in sight, looking pretty happy, talking to some people near a fountain. The other Norm was a painter and a language poet, known to have been living in relative health and joy, and with numerous lovers, while HIV+, for decades.

J did feel a little spooked by the openness of it all.

It had to be how it had to be, the lover was saying. And it helped keep things really hot—there was that, too. The conversation went back to boats.

Someone startled J with a tap on the shoulder.

"Did you find your mom?" It was the *Real Humans* woman. J blushed.

"Look," the woman said. "I can see you're disgusted by us."

"What?" J said.

"I know about young people. They're very conservative and very judgmental." She had now opened up her speech to the whole group, but she was still clearly addressing J. "You think we're all decayed and dying, which we are, of course, but you're dying every day, too. You'll just keep dying and dying. I know from my own children." She took a sip from her little blue drink. "I mean, look at you. Quiet as a superior little mouse."

"Let me get you some water," M said to the woman.

"No, no," she said. "I don't need water. I'm just saying something about this young woman. She's had her little bit of success. She's thinking to herself, I'm not going to make the mistakes these people made. I'm going to keep my head down and work and not hurt anyone's feelings too much and not get hurt myself. She thinks she's solved it all with her preemptive gloominess and her inoffensiveness."

"You should enjoy your party," the man who had lived on a boat said.

"There's a subspecies of these young people," the woman

was saying. "They're very careful. The young women espe-cially; they're the worst—"

"You're so right," Q said. She took hold of Real Humans's arm. "They are the worst. This one's probably innocent enough, though."

"She's a wily mouse, you don't know. Do you have chil-dren?" she now asked Q. "They're very judgmental. If you have children, you know."

"This one's kind of my daughter."

She gave Q the once-over. "Yes, they're all kind of our daughters, aren't they?"

"I wouldn't take any of this too seriously," Norm's lover said to J. "She's been starting arguments at parties for thirty years. Haven't you?"

"For fifty years," Real Humans said.

"Did you hear about Gene Hackman?" Q asked.

"He doesn't really live here," Real Humans said. "He lives one island over. I heard he's doing just fine."

"I feel kind of elated," J said.

"Sure you do," Real Humans said.

It was as if Q's secret wasn't that she'd lost her home, or lost her money, or was secretly ill, but that she actually knew what she was doing. Or maybe she had lost her money, and her home, and maybe she was ill, but she was able to handle it. All these partygoers seemed able to handle their lives.

"He was just scratched up a bit," Norm's lover said.

"Who was scratched up?"

"Gene Hackman. He wasn't really hurt at all."

"That's what I thought," Q said. "I thought he would be fine."

Everyone admired Gene Hackman.

"Hasn't he had a sad life?" J asked. "I thought I'd been told that. That his mother had died in a fire started by her own cigarette?"

No, no, his life had worked out. He had a great life. He joined the navy. He was a failure in acting school. When his old teacher saw him working as a doorman in New York, the teacher said that he'd always known he'd amount to nothing. He was retired from movies. He had three kids. He had paired up with an underwater archaeologist to write three adventure novels. Maybe four adventure novels. Or one was a Western, maybe. It was titled *Justice for None*.

ONCE AN EMPIRE

DREAM · EMPIRE

I'm a pretty normal woman, maybe even an extremely normal one. Especially now as I'm entering my mid-thirties, which are among the most normal of years. I live—I used to live, that is—in a small lofted studio apartment on the top floor of a six-story building on a tree-lined block, across the way from an abandoned police station. I bought that studio with an inheritance from, well, it doesn't matter from whom. I bought it because it was time. My mother no longer tenderized meat with a hammer, I had failed to become the cabaret singer or CEO she once might have become; the termination of our roommatehood had become essential. This was many years ago. I love my apartment so much. Its window looks out onto the Jehovah's Witness Watchtower building whose enormous lightbulb billboard broadcasts the temperature in Fahrenheit, the time, then the temperature in Celsius, then the time again, then the updated temperature in Fahrenheit, and so on, unto eternity. Having sight of that billboard: it used to make me feel like neither time nor temperature would ever change without first petitioning my approval.

As a normal, stable adult with an ordinary life on a quiet street in a peaceful neighborhood, I never thought I'd be the victim of an especially unusual crime. Or of any crime, really. If it was a crime. A middle school counselor once told me that she didn't know if as a child, she was, or wasn't, beaten with a belt one or many times because, she said, we never really know what happened in the past. Only what we dread or long for in the future. And often not even that, she added. OK, sure.

It was a Tuesday when what happened happened.

Every Tuesday night I go and see whatever is playing at the movie theater nearby. I'm not choosy. I'm happy to see whatever everyone else is going to see. That way I stay in touch without having to talk to people, which is great, because even though I very much like people in general, I find most people, in specific, kind of difficult. I prefer the taciturn company of my things. I love my things. I have a great capacity for love, I think.

Like the movie theater. I love the popcorn there, which makes me feel ever so slightly asthmatic. And I love the heavily patterned carpet that recalls the slot machine section of a gas station out West. And that fateful Tuesday evening I saw a movie that was *about* love. If also about Japan, and kind of about dinnerware, too. The movie ran late, past midnight, which is when—this is what they said in the movie anyhow—the veil between the living and the dead is at its thinnest.

Its being the witching hour didn't spook me, I want to be clear about that. One time the Watchtower displayed a static LL:LL, and *that* spooked me, but little else has ever spooked me. Which is to say, I wasn't out of sorts that Wednesday morning. (Because now that I think about it, that fateful Tuesday night was actually a Wednesday—as kids we used to call Wednesday hump day—morning.) After that movie I was walking my regular walk home, past the now nineteen months' static construction site that sits at the corner of my very own block, right next to the abandoned police station.

I turned the corner, past the plywood barrier, on around to the front of the abandoned police station. From there I saw the six stories of my own building. I saw my window. My lights weren't on. Which was wrong. I always leave the lights on in my apartment, day or night. I've never shaken that childhood fear that in the dark things cease to exist. Maybe that is what really happens, if briefly; science these days keeps confirming the strangest things.

My window dark: probably just the coordinated demise of several bulbs, I told myself. Or something. Something pretty normal.

I looked down at my feet, as if to remind myself of them. A breeze blew, carrying an ever so slight scent of burning leaves and an industrial shoreline kind of mildew. I felt myself growing dim through inexposure. Maybe a fuse had blown. A very important fuse.

Some sort of sound. I looked back up, toward my unlit window. Some . . . *thing* was emerging from the darkness there. At first, it looked like a nothingness that had acquired an outline on the cheap. But as it descended—it was descending—it became more fully ontologically realized. It was my ironing board.

I'd forgotten that I even had an ironing board. It was an old family thing, all wooden. It used to collapse unannounced, and often. I and a series of dogs had been afraid of it when I was a kid. I'd forgotten it to a closet. I would never have said I cared for it. But when I saw it there on the fire escape, out of its context, a great tenderness unearthed itself, flowing from me to it.

The ironing board's gangly back legs hooked over the fire escape's final edge; its front legs made gentle, almost elastic contact with the sidewalk below. Having landed confident as a cat burglar, the board then continued east. Its progress wasn't awkward or zombielike. It moved supplely, playfully. Kind of like a manatee.

Next, with surprising nimbleness, my brown velveteen recliner climbed down, then passed by me in a stump-legged gallop. My wood-armed Dutch sofa shuffled graceful as a geisha. My desk chair seemed to think it had wheels, which it doesn't. A green-globed desk lamp went by. An ordinary plastic dustpan. A heavy skillet, scorched. My things. They were all heading east. With an enviable sense of purpose. An old set of Russian nesting dolls from my father, the ladder I used to reach my storage loft, a forgotten feather duster (blue), a pine cabinet with round hinges, two high kitchen stools I had painted, one of which had a yellow splatter from another project, which splatter I liked to run my finger across. My dresser whose drawers squeaked just so, a faux-colonial laundry basket, a blur of white dishes; a checkered ceramic vase, downy throw pillows, three folding chairs, a harem of kitchen utensils; a video projector, a yarny bath mat, a striped shower curtain, perky Tupperware labels, a corkboard with its map pins, chewed-on chopsticks, a crystal-like vase that makes a finger look cut in half if held in just the right way. "Stuff" is such a childish word. Sheets passed as if floral ghosts. My books rustled by like a military of ducks. My mother had never liked my books. She'd said they kept me from real life, by which I think she meant men, or money, or both. Always accusing things of precisely the crimes they haven't committed.

The parade of my things, I was almost enjoying it. I didn't hate my life, as it left me.

Then my miniature pink plastic-handled two-tined fork, which has COLORADO ROCKIES engraved on its handle in golden letters and is the surviving half of a souvenir set from a truck stop, and which I've had forever and ever: then she went by. Not even among other silverware. On her own. Amid that witching hour crowd of my life, it was she—she who had shared so many bowls of noodles with me, so many scrapings of extra sugar onto plain yogurt, so many steaks cut by another into tiniest bites, she for whom I would refuse as a child to eat my dinner until she was found—it was for her, my fork, that my heart beat wildest. Until the moment of her exodus, I had been too mesmerized even to think of moving. What I watched felt no more personal than that cartoon movie with the brooms, a movie I'd never much liked because it had no words. But my little fork. I wanted to follow her. To beg her to stay or to ask her why she was leaving. Why didn't I run after her or shout out to her? Why did I feel so limbless? Maybe it was terror; I could barely move. And she—she receded beyond my field of vision, as my old ally the Watchtower did not stutter in telling the time, the temperature, the time again, and the temperature again.

Oh, fork. How does it feel to be a bat? I don't know. Sleepy, maybe? Hungry? Yearning? Content? I don't know how I felt that Tuesday night. Or hump day morning. Whatever it was. I barely even know how I didn't feel. I didn't feel like reading a newspaper, or having a coffee, or going for a jog, or watching television. Nor did I feel like crying behind the boiler in the basement. Or like trying out for something. I didn't even feel like I had lost someone I deeply loved; this was different from that. I didn't feel like going to another movie and asking for extra butter on my popcorn. I didn't feel like talking to someone who would understand.

I managed the short crawl to the stoop of the familiarly abandoned police station and then rested there. Above me: one flagpoled balustrade where surely, at one time or another, a flag had hung. Had that been twenty-one years ago? One hundred and one? I didn't know. Maybe no one knew. An old police station. Hadn't I seen a crime? I smiled, a little. A dew was breaking.

Time had blinked or I had fallen asleep. I saw a few skid marks on the sidewalk, as if from a bicycle. I don't have a bicycle, I thought. I don't think I do. Though I have a toolbox with rubber feet. Or had one. The sun washed out the face of the Watchtower's lightbulb billboard in brightness. Where my window was I could see only reflected light.

Britain, once an empire, now a small island off Europe— that was my thought.

A sound then like the Apocalypse. The superintendent, vacuuming the lobby of my building, with one of the front doors propped open. The super's name sounds like that of a Roman emperor. Advertus, I think it might be. Or Nero. He knocked on the glass of the unopened front door of the building—but you're *inside*, I thought briefly—and waved at me, half friendly-like.

I waved back. Then I beckoned him.

"I've forgotten my keys," I found myself calling out in a childish tone as he crossed the street toward me.

Claudius offered me his enormous paternal hand. After a brief moment of hesitation I realized the hand was to help me stand up, not just to wonder at. "Was there," I asked as casually as I could, dusting off the back of my skirt, "some kind of electrical blip last night?"

"Something happen?" he asked, laughing, showing teeth.

It is in the nature of a dream that we can't stub our toe against it. I was told that more than once, by my mother, or maybe by my father. Inside my apartment, which the emperor kindly opened for me, was only my ancient stuffed animal dog, Jasper. Him, and a stray leaf, and a to-do list magneted onto the refrigerator.

"Did you move? Are you moving?"

I shook my head. "This is a surprise," I said. "I mean, this is terrible."

"Yes," he said, and his lonely word echoed against the high ceiling.

I couldn't tell him what I'd seen the night before. He seemed like a nice guy, but still, I couldn't tell him.

"I'm sure no harm was meant," I said, when Nero insisted I file a police report.

"For the other people in the building," he preached.

He walked me to the station. I knew that if I reported the truth of what I had seen, I'd soon be under the fluorescent light of an intake room at a nearby hospital. Even the most normal person, if placed in a highly abnormal situation, can be mistakenly perceived as the source of the abnormality of the person/circumstance aggregate. I signed a sheet attesting to an inventory of objects. I felt as if *I* had committed the crime. During the brief interview, I broke into tears, though they may have been fake, I'm not sure. I even said, "I feel so guilty!" A hand went to my back; I was told that people forget to lock their doors all the time, that I shouldn't feel bad about being trusting. I would be called were anything learned of my objects, or of my objects' thieves.

I went to eat lunch at a nearby Italian place.

Maggie, one of the waitresses there, knows me as a regular. "You look like you've seen a ghost," she said.

I'd intended to order spaghetti with meatballs. Maybe my eyes watered because Maggie unprofessionally took the seat across from me and patted my hand.

I told her that my apartment was empty.

"You mean you lost somebody?"

I explained that all my stuff was gone. Not just my TV and stereo and cash, but everything. "Lamps, sweaters, my toothbrush, my backup toothbrush, my ironing board. My favorite fork."

"What kind of thief takes everything? That's so weird."

I shrugged. "Or normal. I don't know. Who knows about crime, really?"

"Do you have insurance?"

I said yes, though I didn't know if I did or not.

She gave a little laugh and then pursed her lips, like thinking cartoon style. "Who really loves you?" Maggie asked. "Loves you like crazy. Or like really, really hates you—"

"Besides myself?" I said. "Yeah, no, it's not like that." I sipped some water.

"Have you ever broken dishes?" she asked.

"Sure."

"I mean, out of anger," she said. "I always wanted to do that."

"What's weird," I ventured, "is my stuff just went and walked out on its own."

Maggie was lost in thought, in dish-breaking fantasies maybe.

"Just left," I continued, "like kids running away from home—"

"I'm sorry," she said to me. "But I have to get back to work. You'll be OK. I promise."

I couldn't refurnish my apartment; I just couldn't. I decided to rent it out. The first prospective tenant said he was a painter, that he liked the light of my apartment, and then he offered me two hundred dollars less than I was asking. "I can see you're a person with a rich interior life," he told me. I suppose he was trying to flatter me as some kind of sponsor of the arts. I'm fine with the arts. But that was not why I agreed to his lower price. I just wanted to cover my property taxes and maintenance fees and have things over and done with.

Myself, I rented a furnished room in a dormitory eleven blocks away. The lessee was a Brooklyn Law School student who was doing something or other in a cold and northern country for a term or two. I could see the Watchtower from the rental room, though I had to lean out the window in order to do so. I went for walks, made smoothies, tried acupuncture, read magazines. I did those things that people do. But the oddness of the furniture crime pressed upon me. Had it changed me? Not that I was so great before, but I had been comfortable with myself, and I had finally escaped an old feeling that I was a failed version of someone—it doesn't really matter who—else. I knew I was still fundamentally my old reliably me-like version of me. And yet I felt as if the real me were out

there somewhere, waiting for my return. I felt wanted by that
real me.

Time passed. Not an item of mine—not a lamp a watch a
fork a chair an antique ironing board, not a thing—was found
at any of the usual fronts where the police, so they said, were
accustomed to finding things. I walked back down to the precinct to ask if they had dredged the river. This was misunderstood as a joke. I think this misunderstanding happened
because I'm a woman. If I were a man, maybe they would have
dredged. Or thought there was something wrong with me for
asking.

Though I no longer went to the movies on Tuesdays, some
new habits settled in. I, like hundreds or maybe thousands of
other people, found myself regularly attending an indoor
crafts and antiques market. Some of the merchants there were
steady, and some switched in and out. One vendor made exquisite benches out of salvaged wood. Another used old
books to make bookshelves. A third sold knit gloves, with the
letters for ANGEL stitched onto the fingers of one hand and for
DEVIL stitched onto the fingers of the other. Naturally there
was also well-packaged jam. Often it was hard to tell who
was running any particular stand, as there were no assigned
places where vendors stood, and vendors wandered away from
their posts, to visit other vendors, I guess, so one (or I at least)
was left with the impression that these things had brought
themselves out to the market of their own free will.

Of course I hoped *my* things would turn up. Set themselves out for sale, just like people do, kind of. A normal
fantasy, really, given the circumstances. It didn't happen.
Nevertheless, I was often happy there at the market, for spans
of time as long as fifteen minutes. I felt like I was thumbing
through all the lives I wasn't leading but might have led. One
where I wore dresses that looked like they were made out of

doilies and old satin; another where I had a special wood holder for my milk bottles; and a third where I was a typesetter or just collected typesettings. I imagined all the people these objects had owned: short people, and fat people, and people who thought periwinkle was purple, and those who thought of it as blue, and people who blamed their mothers for everything that went wrong in their lives, and people who genuinely liked wearing pearls. Such a crowd.

Each weekend, on my way back from the market to my rented room, I'd pass by an empty lot with three dumpsters on it. The term "dipsy dumpster" then always popped into my head. So I'd think about that term, and then I'd think about how it was a strange term, and I'd wonder where we neighborhood kids had gotten it. Then I'd think about the girl who'd lived across the street from me when I was young, and who had brain damage from being thrown around by an alcoholic dad when she was a baby, and who was beautiful and whose adoptive parents had changed her first name when they got her at age four, and that girl, in addition to saying "dipsy dumpster," used to say "nekkid" instead of "naked," which really bothered me, even though we mostly had a great time together. That same little sequence of thoughts ran through my mind each Saturday as I passed those dumpsters. Like a gentle bull within me helplessly charging at the sight of red.

One Saturday—the face of the Watchtower was obscured by fog—as I walked past the dipsy dumpsters, steeled for the predictable memory assault, an unexpected rush of happiness came over me. The happiness arrived earlier than did any perception that might claim responsibility for it. Then, preemptively overjoyed, I noticed my miniature two-tined fork. The pink-handled one. With its slightly melted plastic, and the gold filament mostly missing from the RAD part of COLORADO ROCKIES. It was just there, on a little side table near the first dumpster. My mom had bought that fork for me when we were on a road trip, I was remembering. The fork hadn't originally been alone; it had been part of a souvenir set that also included a spoon, a spoon that maybe still persisted somewhere. My mother had bought me that tiny silverware the day after we'd seen enormous sequoia trees. She'd liked my hair that day; she'd set it back in two braids so tight that they gave me a kind of languorous headache. It hadn't been a particularly important day, that fork-buying day. I don't know why I'd forgotten it or why I was suddenly remembering it. It was just a pretty nice day. We had been pleased with each other. I really loved that fork.

I stepped toward it. I was debating internally whether or not to touch the little fork, to test her reality in that way. Then I saw, near the middle dumpster, among other things, a blue kitchen stool that had a spackle of yellow paint, a spackle that I recognized with horror. Folded neatly over that stool was a pale blue gingham quilt of mine, the one that had nearly smothered me. Turning just a few degrees, I found myself faced down by my old ironing board. My armchair, my striped cardigan, my old yellow toaster . . .

I heard voices. Two men were carrying my dining table. The taller one, an orange-haired man with black-rimmed glasses and tight dark jeans, seemed to be the one in charge.

"Nope, it's not my stuff," he proclaimed. "I'm just helping. She's bringing her truck round to load up for the day."

"This is the dipsy dumpster," I said. The phrase was assailing me.

"There's good space here"—he gestured widely—"to pull in for loading."

"She bought this stuff, or she's selling it?" I asked Tall, in a voice as gentle as I could muster, one that I hoped came across as tenderly demanding.

The lesser man had walked away; he was gesturing to the taller man to join him. "I guess I'm not the person you should talk to," Tall said with finality, but standing still, as his companion looked on, irritated, waiting. I wanted Tall to choose me over Lesser. "I think this is what didn't sell, but I really don't know."

"Huh." So they were unwanted, my things. Excellent. Fortunate. I continued to stand still. Tall also stayed still. Did the vendor—She—look like me? I didn't ask. Very quietly and calmly I asked instead, "Well, what about . . . well . . . do you know . . . the price of that itty-bitty fork over there?"

Two dollars, he said. I asked after the quilt. He said he believed it was handmade by a coterie—he used that term, "coterie"—of older women in a small town in Louisiana. He believed she was asking $160 but thought I could probably get it for $140.

Lies don't bother me much; that wasn't the thing. What saddened me was that these things had tried to make it on their own and had failed. I set myself up, alone, on one of the blue kitchen stools and waited for her. Whoever She was. Whatever truck She might be driving. The Watchtower's face remained obscured, so I don't know how time passed, or how much of it did. Time can be the ultimate in fickleness, the ultimate in reliability. A white pickup truck did eventually reverse into the lot. A woman, yes, emerged from the driver's side. She had lusterless blond hair and prominent teeth, and if She had begun to whinny, it wouldn't have surprised me much. "Disappointed" is not the right word, but it's neighborly with it.

"You shouldn't leave your stuff just out here, like old milk cartons," I chastened.

She didn't look grateful for the advice.

I pulled out my checkbook.

"I only take cash," she informed me chewingly.

"I intend to get lots of things." More if she had more. She couldn't take a credit card? But surely she'd wait for me while I ran out to an ATM?

"No. Won't wait."

"Really?"

"It's cash now or cry."

Maybe I should have been kinder upon our initial introduction. Or meaner. "Were you even in the market today? I was there. Aren't you here to sell things? Aren't you a seller? I'm a buyer. Isn't it exactly me that you spend your life hoping to meet?"

"I need to get home," she said, shrugging. "I live in New Hampshire."

"No, you don't."

She stared at me. "I'll probably be back next weekend." A pause then. "I expect I'll have more quilts."

I didn't hate that woman. I really didn't. Truth be told, I was gaining some much-needed perspective. Distance, it's sometimes called. She's a small potato, I was thinking. If I bide my time, if I quietly observe, if I seek the expertise of others, I can find the man behind it all. Wasn't that the way it was in the movies? You gathered information patiently. You didn't pounce right away. I walked into the Seventy-eighth Precinct police station with my just reclaimed fork and pale blue blankie in hand.

A man there, at a desk.

Uniforms make me think of people as things, which is by no means necessarily a denigration.

"What was the vendor's name?"

She was just out by the dumpsters. I didn't get her name. She had horse teeth.

The man sighed with genuine emotion. It made his chest heave in, and out, then in and out again, more softly. I hadn't really been looking at him. But that gentle sigh made me notice him. Tall and softly formidable—tubby, I guess—with a buzz cut and a face that seemed very drawable.

"Let's go back to the beginning," he murmured without judgment. "Tell me where you live."

His eyes were beautiful and gray-green. He was, somehow, very *real*. Maybe the uniform contributed to that. He emanated unarticulated hopes and maybe suffering and fear and maybe a great capacity for love, even an ability to love things he had not yet known for years and years. Mister Pretty, I dubbed him. Mister Real Pretty.

"Miss? I was asking for your home address?" A hint of impatience.

My mom—she would have frowned upon my interest in a police officer. Or been far too excited about it. It struck me that I could offer to take him to bed, to that strange bed in my pretend dorm room rental, in my wrong life. They've done studies on these things, and they say that most men happily agree to such offers.

"Do you live near here?" I asked, in turn.

He seemed not to hear that, or able to pretend not to have heard it.

"Do these Wanted posters"—I went on—"ever really solve anything? These people, they all look the same."

"Can we focus, ma'am? Your address." I didn't say anything. "Unfortunately, we've got loads to do here, and weekends are understaffed, so if we could get these basics filled out as quickly as—"

But when love is real, there's no such thing as Time. I wasn't the criminal, was I? I wasn't Wanted. Mistakes could be made, though. Misidentifications. But one must be treated with respect regardless. I've had so many bad ideas in my life. I needed to be a new woman.

I knew I couldn't give him my address. Not my former address, and certainly not my current one. It would just make it that much easier to find me. Even if this guy in particular was absolutely trustworthy, an angel. Still, things could get . . . out of his hands. I had just begun to reclaim my life. I held my fork and quilt closer. I would never give my address out again. At no time and at no temperature. And if they somehow got my new address anyhow, I would keep on moving.

"I'm sorry to have taken your time," I said to that man, with longing, and anger, and regret, and resolve. "I really am so sorry."

I stepped back out into the salubrious cold. My mom. I knew where she lived. Or used to live. When had we last spoken? Had we argued? She had never even seen that studio where I had lived so happily for a long time. There were so many things that we had in common. Even owned in common, kind of. She might have advice for me. I wouldn't necessarily have to take it. I could put my hair in braids. I could stay with her awhile.

ACKNOWLEDGMENTS

Willing Davidson provided essential editorial advice for almost all of these stories; I am likewise indebted to Eric Chinski, Carin Besser, Deborah Treisman, Claire Gutierrez, Ben Metcalf, Joanna Yas, and Jared Bland. The literary agent Bill Clegg has also been a wonder. I am furthermore grateful for the support of the Dorothy and Lewis B. Cullman Center for Scholars and Writers at the New York Public Library, the Mary Ellen von der Heyden Fiction Fellowship of the American Academy in Berlin, and the Hald Hovedgaard Danish-American Writers' Retreat.